A. Willow Evans

Week In My Knees

A. Willow Evans

# Week In My Knees

## It's Haunting. It's Hair-Raising. It's Hot.

JustFiction Edition

**Impressum/Imprint (nur für Deutschland/only for Germany)**
Bibliografische Information der Deutschen Nationalbibliothek: Die Deutsche Nationalbibliothek verzeichnet diese Publikation in der Deutschen Nationalbibliografie; detaillierte bibliografische Daten sind im Internet über http://dnb.d-nb.de abrufbar.
Alle in diesem Buch genannten Marken und Produktnamen unterliegen warenzeichen-, marken- oder patentrechtlichem Schutz bzw. sind Warenzeichen oder eingetragene Warenzeichen der jeweiligen Inhaber. Die Wiedergabe von Marken, Produktnamen, Gebrauchsnamen, Handelsnamen, Warenbezeichnungen u.s.w. in diesem Werk berechtigt auch ohne besondere Kennzeichnung nicht zu der Annahme, dass solche Namen im Sinne der Warenzeichen- und Markenschutzgesetzgebung als frei zu betrachten wären und daher von jedermann benutzt werden dürften.

Coverbild: www.ingimage.com

Verlag: JustFiction! Edition ist ein Imprint der
LAP LAMBERT Academic Publishing GmbH & Co. KG
Heinrich-Böcking-Str. 6-8, 66121 Saarbrücken, Deutschland
Telefon +49 681 37 20 310, Telefax +49 681 37 20 310-9
Email: info@justfiction-edition.com

Herstellung in Deutschland:
Schaltungsdienst Lange o.H.G., Berlin
Books on Demand GmbH, Norderstedt
Reha GmbH, Saarbrücken
Amazon Distribution GmbH, Leipzig
ISBN: 978-3-8454-4526-7

**Imprint (only for USA, GB)**
Bibliographic information published by the Deutsche Nationalbibliothek: The Deutsche Nationalbibliothek lists this publication in the Deutsche Nationalbibliografie; detailed bibliographic data are available in the Internet at http://dnb.d-nb.de.
Any brand names and product names mentioned in this book are subject to trademark, brand or patent protection and are trademarks or registered trademarks of their respective holders. The use of brand names, product names, common names, trade names, product descriptions etc. even without a particular marking in this works is in no way to be construed to mean that such names may be regarded as unrestricted in respect of trademark and brand protection legislation and could thus be used by anyone.

Cover image: www.ingimage.com

Publisher: JustFiction! Edition
is an imprint of the publishing house
LAP LAMBERT Academic Publishing GmbH & Co. KG
Heinrich-Böcking-Str. 6-8, 66121 Saarbrücken, Germany
Phone +49 681 37 20 310, Fax +49 681 37 20 310-9
Email: info@justfiction-edition.com

Printed in the U.S.A.
Printed in the U.K. by (see last page)
ISBN: 978-3-8454-4526-7

# Prologue

Tonight was probably one of the most horrible nights I have ever had- it was the night that me and Shane were most likely to break it off. I could feel it. But then...I was positive that I wanted him out of my life when he told me what he did.

"Are you kidding me? Are you fucking serious?!" I yelled at him over the bass of the music. We were at a party, and were fighting like always- but this time, it was different. This time he told me that he cheated on me. I didn't curse at him all the time, but cheaters? No- what he didn't understand was that I didn't *deal* with cheaters.

"Yeah, Scarlett! What dah hell? You fink I'm lying?" His drunken drawl of his voice slurred violently at me as he glared at me with such intensity that it almost burned through me. He wasn't looking at his 'Letta' anymore- he was look at Scarlett, his new-found ex. He stumbled a little trying to stand still, sloshing drips of his beer onto his shoes- I didn't like beer and that was the only thing at the party that they were serving so I didn't drink that night.

"Go to hell!" I shoved him away from me- just because he was drunk, and he may have done something stupid didn't mean that I would allow him to make this seem like my fault again. I wasn't going to let him take advantage of me ever again- not after I am finished with him anyways.

"Pa-lease! Like you...like you could ever live without me?! Just...go!" he threw his hands up and pointed a bony finger at me and belched. His eyes blazed and my eyes teared from all my bottled up anger that I have been keeping in for so long.

"Fuck off!" I turned quickly and started speed walking down the hall way, past all the couples that were making out and drinking, with beer cans in their hands, clinking them together and hiccupping and giggling like it was New Years Eve.

\*\*\*

"Scarlett, what happened last night?" both Ivy and Sarah were leaning in on their elbows, just killing themselves dying to know.

I didn't speak. Long pause...

"But it's okay if you don't want to tell us," Sarah sighed and made a pouty face at me. She wasn't one to push me, but of course- that never stopped Ivy.

"Actually no, come on, who else are you ever going to tell about what happened? Why keep it all bottled up when you can tell us," she patted my arm and I sighed, sending that familiar flicker in her eyes. She knew she had me there, *"Please?"* she said in a whiny voice, the sound of it pushing me to insanity. "Pretty plea-"

"Alright! That's enough- I broke up with Shane because he said that he cheated on me! Is that what you really were *aching* to hear?!" I slammed my arms down on the table, fists in place, my hair flamed bright red today as if to show my heating anger.

They gasped and threw their hands to their mouth. To them, I was in the best relationship on campus- me and Shane were *the couple* on campus. They wouldn't in their right minds think that would happen. Ever.

"He was being a jerk to me, so I didn't take any more of it. In my eyes- I don't deserve to be treated like shit, let alone be cheated on." Double gasp from them.

"No one does." I had my temples in my fingers, feeling a raging headache coming on from the reoccurring memories that ran through my head.

1

"He cheated on you?....that bastard!" Ivy was fuming, and she pounded her fist on the lunch table as well. No one looked at us and our banter because we were outside- and it was always noisy outside. Thank god that they held lunch out here all the time. Ivy jumped in her seat like she sat on a pokey object and then smiled like she had an idea.

"We totally have to show him up- let him know what he has been missing."Sarah and Ivy nodded, grinning ear to ear- they loved guy missions. They didn't tolerate the idea of women getting disrespected, and they thought that sex-appeal was one of the best weapons being a woman.

"I don't really feel up to seeing him again and have to battle him out with words. Again. It creates migraines and headaches." I flicked a finger at my head to show my point.

"Well it's not like you're going to get any other chance but now to show him up. Rip the band-aid off when the wound is fresh! I don't really know a plan of what we're going to be doing anyways- Ow! What the fuck, Cody?!" Cody Foreman caught the sleeve of his jacket on Ivy's hairpin, pretty much yanking her pony tail to a pulp.

"Oh, well, *Sorry*! I just caught my jacket on a leaning tower of hair products. You should say sorry to the jacket!" he bellowed a laugh at Ivy's death glare. When someone messes up her hair or make-up, she was rigid. "Now whats this of a plan?" he ringed his hands together, eyes lit up at the thought of mischief.

"None of your chest hair, asshole!" she was squinting at him as if trying to turn him into a neut forever with her eyes. She grinned and I could swear that her eyebrows curled with meanness in them. "Oh, that's right. You have none." then she giggled devilishly at her own joke.

"Oh, that's cold." Then he started grinning and raised a tan eyebrow, "But you have enough for the both of us!" He sighed and then made a bored expression and started to walk off, "I'm getting bored with this- maybe over tea the next time?" He swung around, walking backwards, "Pip-pip! Cheerio, Love!" he said in an imitated British accent, waving with a pageant hand perfectly cupped.

"Something fell out of his pocket, Ivy- go get it! Before he notices!" Sarah whispered loud at her pointing at a crisp white envelope that fell under a table by some guy's conversed foot.

Ivy ripped her loud heels off her feet and threw them under our empty table in the out-door cafeteria and tip-toed over by the guys foot and whispered "Move!" to him. She didn't see his face- just really long brown hair and a beautiful face that couldn't be touched is all I saw, though. He must be a new kid because I don't think I know him, but I don't know half of these people anyways so...

He lit a cigarette and puffed it in her face and snickered. He moved his foot though and I guess that's all that mattered. She snatched it up and ripped a paper out of the envelope. She scanned it.

"Scarlett...looks like your gonna go partying."

She raised a brow and clucked her tongue.

2

# Chapter 1

I walked down the alley, purse in hand. My mini skirt short, making my legs very cold – of course it made them ten times even colder considering I was stupid enough to wear a skimpy skirt on a winter night. Since it's what the invitation told the girls to wear.

It was snowing and as the snow fell on my face the little snowflakes dissolved and burned. The more the flakes fell the redder my face got.

I was standing outside the club with a flashing, neon sign with 'Skinny Jeans' printed in big swirly letters on the front. I sure hated fads. I looked to my right and found some big scruffy guy outside with a drink in hand and a lit cigarette in the other, I looked to my left and found a couple standing close together – obviously trying to get warm. They looked like icicles standing there huddled up. I got the impression that the young rosiness of their faces, they were under-aged. I felt sympathy for them, for they looked like they weren't expecting a ride anytime soon. I had the same situation. The slight difference was that I came here with my ex and his friends and he was inside. I have to say I wouldn't call him my friend, but he was my ride due to carpool. We had a big fight two weeks ago, and that pronounced us from 'Best Couple on Campus' to 'Split'.

His name was Shane. At first, when I just met him, he seemed really sweet. I remember sitting under the cherry blossom tree, sneaking peaks at him through my short and spiked, burgundy hair. I remember how my cheeks got hot when I thought he noticed that I was looking at him. I have known him ever since I enrolled at Cardinal Capri Collage. He had short spiky black hair, square-rimmed glasses and a very nice smile that followed. I can just remember that day in the lounge sitting with Sarah and Ivy,

"I can't believe you fell for that nerd- just look at him, his outfit sets off my nerd-alert scale screaming. I mean seriously, he's not as hot as Brett Lennon." Ivy threw her hands in the air for more of a point.

"At least she likes someone! And you thought she was going to be a lonely cat lady, but I kept telling you, if she's ready to love someone she will, but you didn't listen," Sarah sighed but gave me a little smile, "I think he's nice, I'm glad you found someone Scarlett." She nibbled at her granola bar, shyly looking at her hands like she usually does.

"I didn't fall in love with him, I just have a tiny crush on him is all…" my voice faded expectantly. Everyone at this table knew I had a secret obsession for that boy ever since I started at CCC.

"Well there is only one thing we can do- Sarah?" she looked sideways at her with a sneaky smile on her face, her brow raised.

"Why, I'd love to Ivy." Sarah had a huge grin on her face. Their faces were identical when they both smiled at the same time- you would have thought that they were twins if Ivy didn't have purple hair and Sarah, blue. They stood up out of their seats and Ivy made her way towards Shane.

I made a mad dash towards the exit, looking behind me again to see Ivy, alone, talking to him. I looked back forward to see where I was running just in time to have my face smash in Sarah's green sweater, her little body blocking the exit. I ran smack into her so hard that I fell back and blacked out.

That day I remember waking up in the infirmary to find Shane sitting there right next to my cot smiling a crooked grin. If only I knew what I was getting myself into then.

I shivered and dug in my purse for my phone. 12:10. I was not about to go back in there just to see the way Shane has changed drastically- how he drinks and has tattoos now, how he isn't sweet to me anymore, how he has spiraled out of control through the years. When he is drunk he worries me and frightens me a little bit- he became that way slowly, I don't understand what came over him – but the happy, warm and fuzzy feelings soon went away. I walked across the street in frustration. My red heals clicking their way prominently as if to show how mad I was.

*Clack, clack, clack!*

I thought that I heard footsteps behind me. I slowed down very gradually, trying my best to not click so loud.

Another low sound was playing in the back round right behind me. I could slightly make out another sound of a shoe…

*Tap, tap, tap…*

I rounded the corner, took off my heels and full out ran, barefoot, trying to find the closest convenience store.

*Smack, smack, smack!*

My feet burned with cold sensations boiling through my legs. I was sprinting as fast as I could, but found no convenience store in sight. I winced severely when I slid on some ice but still safely found myself running on rough pavement again. I stopped just in time to hear an obvious, hard, boot-like clunk in the slush and snow about a couple yards away.

*Tap…tap…tap…tap…tap!…tap!…tap!…*

I ran into the nearest place I could see. I slammed the door open and felt the hot tears running down my face, blurring my vision. I saw many colors, bright reds, dark browns, blacks, greens, yellows. I felt the tension in the air, and the smoke on my face. It smelled like burnt pizza, cigarettes and cigar smoke. I could hear mumbling and clacking of pool balls. I turned around to meet a man's big, bright blue eyes through my blurry-teared eyes.

That was all I could see of him..

# Chapter 2

"What the?"I looked up to see I was in a room. A dark room and I was pretty sure it reeked of perfume. I acted like I was still sleeping and didn't move, but took in my surroundings. I flipped my body on my back to see up at the ceiling. Then I noticed that really familiar beige stain on the ceiling. I remembered that stain like it was the back of my hand. That was the night when my mother left my dad. I vividly remember the flashing colors going through my mind – the pink sequin dress, the baby blue tuxedo, the red drink in my mom's hand the green drink in my dad's. I remember them screaming at each other. My mom got so angry that she grabbed the nearest perfume bottle and tried to chuck it at him only having to throw it up at the ceiling with bad aim.

I slowly sat up and could faintly smell bacon and heard the sizzling of the frying pan down the hall. I rubbed my head and looked down – I was still wearing my mini skirt and tank.

"Damn." I looked all around me and saw I was in my Mom's room. The birds were chirping and the sliver of light was coming in the blinds. I opened the blinds and was blinded by white, sparkling sunshine. It was like god covered the outside in white rich fabric in my front yard. Then I could hear voices.

"Well, it isn't like her to get drunk, I just don't know what was going through that mind of hers! Seems Shane must have really done something to get her so upset…" My Mother's voice poured out of the kitchen hallway leading to the bedroom. Sweet, but sounded worried as hell. "I'm just so glad you brought her home, err, Romeo," I could hear the sincere smile in her voice.

"Your Welcome, Miss Todd, it's nice to know that she is safely home," he sounded relieved. "So, uh, who is this Shane?" The wicked curiosity in his voice clearly eager, and I could hear the smile in his voice.

"Nice boy…well was a nice boy…" She sounded somber, like it was a great tragedy that she couldn't bare to speak of. "I don't know what has gotten into him these days, its like he's not well…him anymore, It's like he's not that sweet kid I knew him as, back a year or two ago, not the paper boy who always hand delivered it special to my door. He would always ask if Scarlett was around…always wondering if she was busy or needed help with their chemistry homework…." Her voice trailed off, a sad chuckle trickling out of her lips.

"Well that's…odd, I can say." I could hear his teeth clink against a lip ring while he spoke. Even though he sounded concerned I could just make out the hint of humor in his voice. "Well, what a pity that mankind had to put such a young potential human being to waste, what a shame…" I heard him chuckle under his breath. Ugh! When I see him I'm gonna-

"I should check to see if Scarlett is awake, I'll be right back," Then I heard muffled out footsteps walking their way to the bedroom. I flopped myself on the bed and threw the covers over my head. It's not like I didn't want her to know I was awake…I just didn't need to get her wrath with this hard hangover kicking in. The door creaked open and I heard the little *Clunk-scratch-scratch* of her slippers on the hard wood floor.

"Honey, are you awake?" She walked over to the side of the bed and lifted the covers to see my head. I acted like I was waking up and said in a groggy voice, "Mom?"

"You didn't tell me that you met a new friend. Explain. Now." I could hear that she was upset. Great.

5

"New friend?" I let my eyebrows push together like I was confused. I usually did this to save myself from her nagging whines and yells.

"Don't mess with me Scarlett. You remember this boy fine and well- and you're going to tell me how you met him. You better have a damn good answer why you got so drunk too. Explain yourself!" Okay now she was really pissed, even better to put on my list of things to deal with along with a soon pounding hangover.

"Okay, okay I'll tell you everything but can you lend me some clothes to wear considering we're the same size?" I raised my eyebrows at her, I knew she was definitely not going to let me walk out there in my slutty looking clothing and bed head, along with my eye liner and mascara smeared all over my face.

"Fine." She started digging around in her walk-in closet, I could hear the sound of *Clunk-scratch-scratch* on the floor, along with the sound of metal hangers falling to the ground. Then she threw a long-sleeved, velvety, red blouse at me along with some dark wash jeans that I left at her house last weekend. "That will do, now go in the bathroom and clean yourself up. We have guests over, and you better hope he doesn't leave soon because I'm going to have a little talk with you later." she gave me the death stare and then painted a smile on her face and headed toward the kitchen muttering to herself.

I hopped in the shower and let the hot water run down my face. I was so lightheaded that I sat down in the shower and just let the water run over me. I sat there for what seemed like hours but turned out to be minutes. I got out of the shower and I looked at myself in the mirror.

I looked like a mess. Mascara run down my face and my auburn hair looked more purple than usual, it looked purple-red. I looked at the person in the mirror with a look of new. This was me. This is how people see me, and this is how see myself.

But that's going to change.

I rapped a towel around my torso and then dried my hair with a different one. I put my clothes on and then straitened my hair like usual, even though my hair is already ridiculously flat. I wash my face and then put on mascara and tips of eyeliner at the corners of my eyes. I looked in the mirror at my spiky-tipped reddish-purple hair. I looked good, making the person in the mirror smile at me.

I cleaned up my things and then left the bathroom, walking my way to the bedroom. I could hear the clink of a coffee cup and forks against plates along with hushed talking. I laid my toiletries on the bed and made my way out to the kitchen.

He looked up at me with his big black, eyeliner rimmed eyes through his blackish-brown hair and grinned, all teeth - making his lip ring curve in. He took a long sip of his coffee and then sat it down looking at the table smiling to himself. "Good morning." he mumbled and then looked up at me with a curious look of mischief playing a smile on his face. I smiled a falsely back at him and moved over to the green cabinets, opened the one, grabbed a glass and set it down on the counter making my way over to the fridge to get some orange juice. "Good morning."

"Would you like to say thank you to Romeo?" her mom looked at her with a tight smile, not succeeding to hide her glare. He face was filled with mixed emotions, resulting with a screwed up expression that made me want to laugh so hard. I had to gulp down my orange juice in order to keep from spitting in all over her and the counter.

I choked down the orange juice in time not to make her smell like citrus for the next couple weeks and said as sweetly as could-

"Why, thank you for bringing my drunk ass home." I smiled sickly sweet at them. He looked at me and said back with as much smart-ass as I did-

"Why it was no problem, Scarlett, but I wasn't the one to take you home though." He gave me a sweet look batting his bright blue eyes at me.

"Who took me home then?" I growled back narrowing my eyes at his clean complexion.

"Shane did." He looked at my mother "Oh I forgot to tell you? Shane brought her home not me, I was just the one to walk in and say that I could give her a ride home, but he said that she could just crash at his place, but thankfully I changed his mind into taking her home."

My mom looked at him with an incredulous look - painted face completely gone, and before she could say one word he cut her off abruptly, "I think I should really be going Ms. Todd I really don't want to waste *any* time for you two to talk, that would be a sin of mine, now wouldn't it? Well thank you very much for breakfast," and then he got up and left out the back door and walked away.

No one moved, it was completely silent.

I just stood there leaning against the counter with my mouth hanging open, while my mom was staring at his plate, a look of shock on her face.

"What the hell just happened?" I didn't move and she didn't speak. She closed her mouth and shook her head, then she got up and left, walking all the way back to the bedroom before shutting the door with a click behind her.

I stood there for a couple minutes and then walked over to the couch, turned on the television and just sat there until I eventually slumped over and fell asleep.

7

# Chapter 3

My dreams aren't usually nightmares- usually I don't have them or they are about my everyday life, but this one...this one scared me and confused me.

"What the hell do you think you're going?!" He grabbed my arm, letting his nails dig in hard, and yanked me back until he had a hold around my body, not letting me move. He shoved me in a room, as I noted that I didn't see his face. The room was fogged with cigarette smoke and had a bunch of women, just sitting there and smoking. I noticed that they had red fingernail marks on their arms. All over their arms. I looked at all of them in horror.

No. No, no, no!

I was scared to death because I haven't seen the man's face - but his voice was crisply familiar.

I walked over to one of the women slowly and cautious, completely breaking down on the inside. Her whole body sagged down in her white lawn chair while she smoked. She had faded blue hair and her natural black hair was just seeping through, though she had her face turned away from me that was all I could see of her, her hair. She had on a short skirt, a tank top, and bangles around her wrist. They clanked every time she lifted her hand to her mouth to take in another puff of tobacco air that was slinking out of the cherry of her cigarette. Her hair was in a really sloppy ponytail having strands of her oily, swirly tresses falling down to the side of her face and the back of her neck, her long, long bangs hanging down in her face lazily.

"You know you're never going to leave, so why bother even trying? We're all going to die in here and he's just going to push us to the side while he picks new targets to take. There's no hope for us, and the sad part is we all know it." She had a fainted, rich, high voice, like Juliet preaching from her balcony. She kept her body tilted away like I wasn't worth looking at. Like I was just another victim. Like I was just another new, frightened face. I put a cold hand on her silk skinned shoulder, he shuddered in return and shook it off with a skinny, bony hand.

"He can't do this forever, he can't live forever, and he's not going to get away with this forever. There is hope... You just can't feel it with all of this depression, pain and aggression," I said in a hushed voice and stood there behind her, hiding in her long shadow.

She halfheartedly laughed a low snickering at me, "Ah, you can hope all you want, but I'm telling you now, don't get your hopes up. I have been here for ten years and at thirty-one, there's just no more to rely on anymore." She chuckled sarcastically "Hey who knows I may just have a husband and kids someday, I may just get a beautiful house and finish collage, I might just get free of this hell hole...Well, I guess everyone can dream." She threw her cigarette on the cement floor and left it there to burn the rest of the way through. She crossed her arms and legs and said in a voice that was super icy, "That man had disciples, we will never leave and he will never be stopped. He has seven different names- did you know that? And guess what - he has not been found for about ten years, still. We thought that he was just another person walking the streets- then after everything happened?" She shook her head, "We were done for- he would have already captured us." she went on in a huff getting angrier and angrier with every word she spit out in front of her, "People in here say that he has been doing this ever since he was 16. He got beaten and sexually abused so he became sick in that head of his. The police are still looking for him. And this one girl, she got him so angry and frustrated that he targeted her friends and family. Now look where she is now." she stood up and turned around.

Oh my god.

Sarah looked at me and her voice was chilling, saying, "You did this to me, Scarlett! Because of you- I have been trapped here for so long! I don't get ten years of my life back Scarlett!" she stepped up closer and got all up in my face, "Don't let us all die, Scarlett, stop him before he gets you and me!" then she started to wailed and cry- falling at her knees, looking up at me with mascara-ran eyes. She let out a wail so loud that I jumped.

I jumped right out of a dead sleep, sweaty, hair stuck to my head, and had tear-stained cheeks, waking up to my mom yelling at me and shaking me. I looked up at her with wide, teared up eyes and fell into her arms, and started to sob. I wailed and balled for about twenty minutes, not getting quieter nor getting calm.

"Oh, honey," she patted my head and ran her fingers through my tousled hair while I lay there in her lap and cried. She sat there and listened - worried and hurt by my scared and disturbed behavior. She listened for a long time, my hurt screams and wails. She laid there on the couch - caressing my hair and just listening- not saying a word, her expression on her face, hurt and ashamed. My screams faltered as time grew and then I fell into a deep, dreamless sleep while my mother sat there and watched over me making sure I was okay as I slept.

# Chapter 4

We woke up earlier that night- it seemed she fell asleep while watching me. I woke up about twenty minutes before she did, and took a shower, while I was getting dressed I could hear the clanging of dishes and the popping of opening the spice jars. I got dressed in some baggy comfortable pajamas and went into the living room, sat down on the couch and dosed off. I was just about to go to sleep when I saw the outline of moms head and heard her voice telling me to wake up. "What? Why? It's a school night." I slumped up on the couch cushion and my body sagged as I tried to sit up.

"Wake up - were going out to dinner tonight, just you and me - and by the way, I called you off from school for a week... I told them that we were going on a vacation to Paris and that to send all your homework in the mail to our address." she sat down on the lumpy couch cushion beside me and looked up at me hopefully, "Honey- you have had *way* too much stress put you the last couple months, all with you and Shane-"

"Me and Shane are just fine, and you don't need to worry about me." My voice snapped back unexpectedly and I suddenly felt like a jerk. "I'm sorry mom...I..." My voice faded.

She gave me a sigh and continued on, "And with what happened with dad and me awhile ago." She looked away, trying to hide her tears. She sniffed an wiped her eyes quickly, hoping I wouldn't notice, looked back at me with a concerned look on her face, "All I am trying to say is that you have had enough, no more, and you are going to take this week to relax and spend some time with your Mama," she smiled and rapped her arm around me, giving me a hug and patting my shoulder, I looked up at her with a small smile and opened my mouth to protest when she interrupted me, cutting me off, " I said *no more stress*, Scarlett. Meaning don't cause stress, and *with that* you are going to relax and not argue. This is relaxing, no-worries week, and you're going to use it! So get up! Get dressed! Because we're going out!" She gave me another heart-wrenching sad smile, "I'm worried about you, Hun." Her voice grew small.

"So...Paris huh?" then we both laughed, something that we haven't heard from each other for a little bit.

I got up to go get dressed and put on a red velvet dress with a cross-line back string making my back and lower back fully exposed. It had tiny spaghetti straps for my shoulders, covering two little lines of my slightly tanned skin. My mom curled my hair so when I looked in the mirror I had big, swirly, purplish-red curls around my face, falling just above the middle of my neck. I looked like one of those women in the movies. I smiled at her, and her purple strapless dress. I looked at the both of us and wondered why my mom wanted us to look so fancy. "Now, honey, I *know* how you don't like him and I'm not too fond of him either-"

"*Mom I'm gonna-*"

"*But, I* know you will think tonight is a blast, no stress, just new people and some fun." she beamed at me and then looked at the both of us in the long, full-body mirror that was hung up in the bathroom, then she smiled a little more. We looked like Arieses, beautiful and classy Arieses.

Then we started heading for the door and I started interviewing her. "Mom, where are we going? And why are we so dressed up?" my curiosity the fueling by the minute.

She just sighed and said "You'll see, just common already," she turned around gave me a sneaky smile and then she put on the jacket that matched her dress, handed me mine, and then handed me my purse.

We headed out into the frigid night - both of our teeth chattering loudly while we made our way through the driveway and out to the bright, blue buggy, with all of the purple and black rose decals rapping all around the little car like a pretty, perplex bow. When we got inside, I did not notice her turned it on before to heat up. It was like we stepped into a cute furnace, all cozy and warm.

We started driving and talking about old memories- the ones where I was a baby and she just started going out with dad. How they had to take a fraternity test and how they didn't know if it was his or not. We talked about how I was a little brat all the time and always went for her phone, and tried to eat her lotion. We talked about how we used to always listen to music together- even when I was in her stomach still, she put the headphones up to her tummy. We talked about how we both had a love of swings at the park- and how she would always swing beside me in the normal swings while I sat and swung in the toddler-baby ones.

We talked and talked for such a long time that I soon thought that we were going to drive out of town, but then we finally stopped at a Hotel. It read "Hanson Hotel" on the front in script writing, the building towering so high above the car that I had to lean forward and cock my head just to look up at it. There were lights on in some windows- lights off in some others.

There was a big sign on a painter's mantle in the front of the skyscraper that read: "Fancy Cotillion, The Hanson Hotel hosts the ball of the year! Schmooze, Eat, Drink, Dance, Have a *Ball!*"

Oh, God.

# Chapter 5

"Mom!" I snapped an annoyed look at her, glaring intensely, "What are you trying to do to me?!" I was shouting at her now, "I'm not *cotillion* material!" I huffed at her making my bangs bounce up like springs, out of my face.

She turned off the car and sat there, then turned to me "Just- trust me, okay? This is going to be good for you and if it means that I have to put you in a fancy dress and meet a boy to avoid you going back into depression, then hell! I'm going to do it!" she was out of breath now, seeming she got what she needed out of her.

"I...I am not depressed." I looked down at my hands and I listened to her voice echo in my mind repeating over and over, *"put you in a fancy dress and meet a boy..."*

I looked up at her abruptly and then narrowed my eyes and said in a voice that wasn't mine, "Who is this 'boy'?" then I glared at her even more, "If you are going to even *try* to tell me that *Shane* is here-

"I said someone *new*, Scarlett, and I don't respect that boy anymore- he treats you like garbage now, and honestly I don't know what he has become these days." she gave me a disgusted look, but I knew it wasn't towards me.

I started to ask her who the boy was again but by the time I snapped out of my thoughts, she was out of the car already walking to the big, double doors.

When we stepped inside the lobby just before the arch about ten feet away from us was a room. The room was ginormous and a color burst spewed everywhere with golds, red, yellows, oranges and counting the men and women in clothing there were also a lot of black and pink swirling around the room dancing, talking, and eating. The whole scene looked glamorous just looking at it. I was awestruck by all of the fancy decor.

The men gathering at one side of the food and punch table and the woman gathering at the other side- the girls were looking at the boys with flirtatious looks while the boys were looking at the *food* with flirtatious looks. The couples on the tiled dance floor were so close that a magazine couldn't fall between their chests, and they all looked loving into each other's eyes while they glided in flowing circles, back and forth, and in the corner you could just make out a part of a young lady's dress coming out of the supply closet door. I didn't realize my mouth was gaping open until I felt my mom tap me and my jaw became sore. She chuckled happily at me.

"So...I guess you changed your mind about leaving, I see," she smiled brightly, and chuckled again. I turned to her and smiled.

"Wow, this looks amazing," I grinned bigger and laughed too. The man who was standing at the podium beside me grinned real big and then picked up his pencil and scribbled something down in his little pocket book on the podium, making me feel evaluated, and I all of a sudden had the urge to stir.

"Who would it be, then?" The middle-aged man gave me a flirtatious smile and I felt like I wanted to be sick. I looked at my mom with an awkward smile, and hid behind her a little bit looking away.

"That would be us, me and my *daughter*," My mother rose a brow, obviously seeing the creepy flirting he was sending my way. "My twenty-two year old daughter and I had reservations at Maison de Lillian for the night." her eyes circled him like a snake, I peered behind her a little bit, trying to catch a glimpse of the shocked man- he wouldn't of thought that I was her daughter with my having all my dad's features.

He coughed uncomfortably, choking on air, "Oh, uh your daughter...Last name please?" His voice went all squeaky as I saw the embarrassment clearly written all over his face.

"Todd." she put her hands behind her back - holding her purse, and creepily smiled at him a little more, I saw a bead of sweat run down his cheek as he looked at his podium- noticing that his list was nowhere in sight.

Muttering to his self as he frantically looked for his list of names, my mother sighed making him look even faster - or at least trying until we were waiting for about two minutes and he found his list of reservations. "Now, who will it be then?" he was flustered and frustrated in the end of all of the mess

"Todd." Her voice ringed firmness and professional power.

He smiled sweetly, catching his breath. "Ah, yes." he rambled off our names with a voice like velvet. God he can recover. "Scarlett Todd, *Marion* Todd?" He rose his blond brow in amusement, "I suppose *your* Scarlett?" he smiled at me and looked at my mother triumphant, "Well, *Marion*, how about I lead you to your table?", he grabbed a couple of menus and walked pass me and my mother pompously, leading us to our left, where I didn't even know there was a restaurant, and steered us all the way to the back of the room where it was most vacant. We came upon a blue marble table with black booth seats. We were the only ones who were in a booth.

The back of the room was dimmed with candles everywhere. It smelled like apples and vanilla, like apple pie Ala mote. He sat us down, and me and mom sat across from each other.

"I'll have your waitress come shortly," he set the menus down on the table and my mother picked one up and started skimming the appetizers.

"Mom, this must have cost you a fortune, why would you take us somewhere so...high class? Because I know you *love* to be fancy," I looked at her with amusement, picking up one of the petite, tiny menus. I wonder who's bright idea was to make the menus out of cloth and thread, because honestly- plastic would be easier. Oh my god, I really am going crazy. I took a sip of my water nervously but still in a happy mood.

"Change is good, once in awhile. So what are you thinking about getting?" I looked at the menu and my eyes bugged out *Caviar?!* What is this? *The freaking Boston Tea Party?!"* I felt my jaw get sore.

"Don't you think that this is a little *too* fancy, mom?" I looked at her, shocked. She just shrugged and kept skimming her menu. I shook off the amazingly expensive prices and looked for the cheapest thing on the menu. Holy crap - *10 bucks!? For croutons?!* I continued looking for the next cheapest thing on the menu that wasn't *salad crackers.*

"What are you getting, mom?" I looked at the luxurious pictures on the menu and my mouth watered, I forgot that I have only drank a glass of orange juice today and that was it.

"Uh... I think I might get the duck, what have you picked, Hun?" She looked at me with a warm smile, her purple dress glittering in the low light. She looked like a pianist star- elegant and divine. "What are you staring at?" she chuckled and smiled with confusion clear written on her face. "Hun?" she tapped my shoulder and laughed.

I jolted out of my thoughts, "Oh, sorry mom...It's just that...well you're really pretty, like *really* pretty." I hugely smiled at her when her purple lipstick glittered from lip gloss, and the corners of her mouth upturned in a smile.

13

"Well, you have the same face as me, Scarlett, so I'm glad you think I'm pretty. Thank you," Her green irises of her eyes glowed brightly with passion and joy. I had a happy sort of envy of her. No this wasn't me- beautiful, sweet, and intelligent. I hadn't paid enough attention to my mother to realize that she is so much more luminous in every way, that she is so much more then I will ever live up to. It was a little hard to admit.

"Ah, well, people can wish," I looked at her with new eyes. I had been so caught up in all my stress about collage and Shane that I didn't look at the smaller and prettier things in life- I didn't give them a chance.

"So, what were you thinking about getting?" mom looked over the little paper ad about "MaisoChe Lilian's great Cherry Cheese Cake!". She looked so enticed with the picture that I was sure she wasn't really paying attention to what I was saying to her. She was reading the text- her eyes moving back and forth, over and over, in little pixie-like swift motions.

"Uh..." I looked relieved at the menu when I finally found the next cheapest price, "Um, I think that I'll get the vegetable beef soup. That's okay with you right?" I looked to her, obviously waiting for a comment, but she didn't answer.

She was looking behind me over my shoulder, and her jaw was dropped. She was gaping with her mouth open and looked like she was genuinely shocked. I feebly tried to get her attention, "Uh...Mom?" I waved my hand in her face and kept calling to her, "*Mom?!*" she awoke from her trance, and shut her mouth with a *click!*

I started to turn around to see what she was gawking at, but then I jumped when she yelled in my ear, "You know! This cheese cake looks yummy! Maybe we should get it!" My head snapped back to her attention, and her loud yells were causing me to get light headed, think about suggesting a mint to her, and making people stare at us.

I looked to my right to see an older family of four all snickering at us, saying things like, "What an embarrassing display!" and "I wonder if they forgot their medication this morning?" and then a bunch of mean laughter. I could feel my face get hot and then I realized that I was already getting up and walking over there before I could stop myself. Like I had no control in me, I swiftly stood up and smoothly waltzed all the way over to their table.

The two which looked to be the parents, who were about sixty years of age, looked at me, surprised, while the other two who looked to be the children of the others, and about thirty years of age kept their heads down regretting that they ever laughed along.

I could hear the whispered cries of my mother behind me saying, "Scarlett! Scarlett, what are you doing? Get back here!", but I didn't care; I just kept walking over to them.

The man with the slick back hair and the neatly combed bushy mustache sat high and tall, looking at me with such propriety it made me want to guffaw at them. The crippled white haired lady looked at me in the same manner. Posture strait, ankles crossed, and her white-gloved hands on her lap. When I arrived at their table, I looked them squarely in the eyes and planted my hands on their tables, leaning in.

"You think that *we* are absurd? *Ha!* I think I saw your *granddaughter* out in the ballroom in the closet- maybe you want to worry about your daughter's virginity instead of laughing at us? Thanks!" The younger two of the four stood up and rushed past me, heading their way to the ball room. I just sauntered back to my table a little proud; my mother's face a mixture of laughter and shock.

14

"Right on, Scarlett!" We both laughed and she gave me a high-five, "Holy crap! You got guts, girl! I raised you well," She beamed at me and we busted out giggling. The other people in the restaurant were giving us funny looks, making us beet red with hollow embarrassment.

# Chapter 6

We finished our dinner and mom stood up and took my hand with a happy look on her face- I just stood up and followed her. "Where are we going?" I laughed and tried yanking my hand out of her strangling grip playfully.

"We, my dear, are going to dance!" My smile immediately disappeared and this time I was really trying to get out of her grip. Damn was my mom strong!

"Mom, no! I *don't* dance in public!" I was shaking my head and tripping from trying to plant my heels on the ground, only to just make dark marks. She kept pulling me effortlessly.

"I have a surprise for you! Quit trying to pull away!" She yanked me so hard that I almost fell flat on my face, but she pulled me up in time so that there wouldn't be an embarrassing scene. She dragged me out to the dance floor, and I swirled around to find that almost everyone was dancing around me- even the snooty looking girls and boys were dancing. The music that was playing was not made for a cotillion and very non-proper. Rock music isn't what I would call classy at all- and it was very disturbing to see all the people in tuxedos and girls in frilly pink dresses head banging.

My mom started spinning me back and forth until I was so dizzy I couldn't tell whether I was running into my mother or some girl dancing behind me. The lyrics were blasting in my head, "Well I'm not paralyzed, but I seem to be struck by you, I wanna make you move because you're standing still..." Finger Eleven was a good band. I planted my feet and stood my ground, standing still, waiting for the room to stop spinning, and once it got balanced the song was almost over, so she took me by the shoulders and spun me one more time.

I was still spinning by the time the song ended and a slow song started to play, and then I landed in someone's arms. Startled I started to apologize to the person's chest because I couldn't really look up at the person or else I would probably rudely get sick on them, I was so dizzy. I stated to pull away so that I could steady myself, but they wouldn't let me go. I started to smell a really familiar cologne on them and noticed that I had my head on the chest of their tuxedo and was swaying with the music with my arms around them.

I relaxed and just went with it- hoping it wasn't some creep or something. His hair was brushing against my face- making my nose tickle. It felt like silk and smelled like mint and cinnamon gum. The song ended with a long low note, and before he let me pull away, he whispered in my ear in a voice that made me freeze...

"Don't be such a smart ass all the time, love, and maybe I would like you better." The clink of his lip ring and the purr of his words almost gave me a whiplash as I yanked my arms away. Before I could look at his face, he spun around and started walking away, his dark brown hair lazily hanging over the collar of his tuxedo. The relaxed sway of his body mocking me – slapping me in the face, as if to yell that I actually danced with Romeo. Who knew that someone with the name of the most romantic, handsome, sweetest guy in drama history was such an *ass*. I spun around and with my eyes like daggers and searched to room for my mother. She was talking to a woman who looked about her age.

I starting clicking away over to where she was standing, their conversation coming into hearing range, "But the market is just horrible, it's like there's no economic tell tale

16

for the reason why everything has gone downhill, just disgraceful, don't you think so?" she was sipping some wine, My mother nodded, and started shaking her head in disgrace.

"Yes, I know, just sad." she searched the ball room, obviously looking for me- and when she saw me stomping toward her she had a guilty look that wrote "Busted" all over her face, because she knew she was in deep trouble. I stopped in front of her and shot my arm towards the door, pointing and gesturing for her to come outside with me. She frowned and told the woman she would be right back. I watched as she head for the door and put my arm back down.

"Don't be surprised if she doesn't come back." The lady nodded understandingly.

"I see."

I shook my head. "You don't know the half of it- trust me." I started walking off to the door but the woman grabbed my arm before I had time to leave.

"But, excuse me miss? I just wanted to say- you look divine, have you ever been into acting?" I looked at her with my brow raised, was she kidding?

"Uh, no- I try to avoid any opportunity to be on a stage and the center of attention. Why?" She let my hand fall, knowing she had my full attention.

"Well, you just remind me of someone I know- I'm sure you would love to meet my son? He's a treat, but I'm sure you will get bought by his charm, all of the prim girls do- but he brushes them away, he's into tough girls who have a lot of heart- oh look at me! I'm babbling again! But I would like you to talk to me some time about getting into it, here's my card." In a sly way she slipped me the card while shaking my hand, her manicured, moisturized hand was really cold. "Give me a call soon." Then she walked off with pride and poise in her step. I took a look at the card.

"Meredith Monroe
Acting and Vocalist Extraordinaire,
Let her make your wildest dreams come true!
787-2657"

I was still stunned that she actually made an offer. What? I mean- Why? Why of all people she would pick me to call about a job?

# Chapter 7

I peered at the door and saw my mother looking down at her shoes, waiting for her fate to come kick her in the ass. Right there I felt guilt and shame wash all over me- I shouldn't have been that hard on her. I walked over and passed her, and heard my mom start to follow me. We arrived outside and halted to a stop. I turned to my mother without looking at her.

"Why?" I heard her sigh but she didn't say anything. I was watching her purple dress come down to the pavement and have the water seep up it, making it more Bordeaux then violet. I still couldn't look at her face, and it was still raining.

"I mean shit mom, I can't just forget everything with Shane just because of a new boy if *that's* what you were thinking!" I looked up at her and felt hot streaks running down my face, knowing that they were teardrops not raindrops. I threw my arms in the air and slapped them back on my soaked dress.

"I mean, what do you...what do you expect? I can't be your perfect daughter all the time! I have too much on my plate right now- I have school work piling up, I have to do mountains of laundry, I am barely getting a C- on all my grades, my boyfriend dumped me for some slut, I hate my dad, I can't sleep! I can't be your perfect little girl all the time- because I am not! I am not your Barbie, Mom!" I was looking down at my shoes and turned to walk but then stopped.

"I'm driving." When I got in the car I grabbed the keys out of her purse and rode home. We were silent the whole time, even when we got to the house. I didn't look at her- I just went in the guest room and went to bed early, in my makeup and dress.

# Chapter 8

I woke up the next morning with my earrings tangled in my hair and my dress tangled in the blankets. I whipped my dress off and looked at the time; it was six in the morning. I ripped the earrings out of my hair and put on the first thing I saw in her closet-a purple silk sundress. I slipped it on ignoring the little voice inside me telling me that this was most likely lingerie, slipped on some flats and started to feel my eyes water, hearing the patter of the rain on the window pane. The house went a-lit with the lighting flashing. It was getting close to spring, I could tell because of all the rain and sleet lately.

I silently ran out the front door, doubting my mother would hear me over the loud clapping of thunder. I could barely see but started running down the street, the rain weighing me down, my feet vibrating with pain and itch as they dug deeper and deeper inside my soles of my flats, slapping hard against the tar. My arms felt like a hundred needles were stabbing deep in the skin, flushing them like Santa's rosy cheeks.

I ran into a park then fell to the grass on my knees, not caring if I got dirty or not. I felt a scream pushing at my throat, and started slamming my fists on the wet, soggy grass. My hands burned and stung when I pounded so deep I hit the frozen soil.

I wanted to scream so badly but nothing would come out, nothing but tears. I stood up, all the mud starting to roll off of me, the rain water making me glimmer in the storm. I looked out into the distance and saw a white tent, and started hearing music. People were jumping around and spinning and I could hear their faint laughter.

I slowly started walking over and saw that there was a *huge* tent with a *huge* group of people dancing in many different ways. I saw a group in the middle dancing to Mexican music of some sort. I stood by one of the big pillars holding up the tent, hiding the best I could and watched at the two in the middle were yelling Spanish at each other, laughing, then started dancing again. It looked like salsa but a lot more...*touchy* than that. They spun around and would shimmy, flip, and shake. When they were finished, a blond girl in tight white shorts and a white tank top, shut off the tape that was playing and then put her own CD in the little slide. A hip-hop Mexican mix started playing, like a merger of somewhere like Spain or Cuba Mixed their music with American. She yelled something in Spanish so fast that I couldn't catch a word that she was trying to say. I mean- I took Spanish but I ended that grade with a C-.

*"Romeo! Mueve el culo por aquí y la danza!"* She started throwing little blue Dixie Cups at the opposite pillar across from me. I peeked over at a tall man who was staring at me through the rain. I slunk back a little further, hoping he was just spacing off but then he cocked his head to the side and started smiling.

*"Nina! Sube el volumen!"* He then ran into the middle of the circle and grabbed her waist. He swung her head back and let her sway back and forth before letting her spin out and crush back into his arms again. They started to circle each other, and he was firmly holding her in place. They stopped and she flung her leg up and started quickly sliding her body toward the floor then he pulled her up into his arms and she started shaking her hips and shimmying. Soon after that he dipped her and let her swing her head back and forth for a little bit.

*"Parece que tenemos un invitado sorpresa."* He gave a devilish grin and then spun her out and back into his arms by the time the song ended.

"*Si?*" Confused, she looked at him with misunderstanding. She fell to the cement square that the tent covered, and started stretching, her shirt riding up to the bottom of her zebra print bra.

"Yes we do, and I am done speaking Spanish for the day- I have done it enough." He smiled at the side of the pillar, tipping his body to the side and waving at me. "*Hola, chica.*"

I slowly slid more far into the crevice of the tree and the pillar, sucking my stomach in as far as I could. "*Ah, no se puede ocultar!*" I stood as stiff as a board and started hearing the first track that they were dancing to the first time play, the salsa beat started in but it started getting more powerful. The others were laughing silently and started mumbling something in Spanish to each other and then giggling some more. "*No entiendo porque te escondes, pobres* Scarlett!" Out of nowhere his hand appeared in front of me, grabbed me and then pulled me out in the middle of the cement floor.

He swung me in his arms so that I had my hand on his shoulder and the other up raised in his hand. "*Estúpida, ingenua Scarlett, todos podemos ver!*" I could finally see who he was under the light of the lamp hanging above us. I gasped, but he didn't move- he just kept standing there.

"What the *hell* happened to your face?" I was gawking at the little red dots, holes, and tiny red cuts.

"I took all my piercings out. Duh." He rolled his eyes, then noticed my get up.

"What the hell happened to me? What the hell happened to *you*?" He examined me up and down, "Not that I don't approve of course," He gave me a smirk and laughed in a low tone. The others joined in with him and belted out their own belly laughs.

I felt myself getting red as the others joined in with him and I yanked my hands out of his grip, noticing that I was sweating in this frigid weather. "Go to hell," I spun around to leave when one of the Mexican men with big black eyes stepped in front of me.

"*Hola*, Scarlett. My name is Hidalgo." he smiled, "Would you like me to walk you home?" When he shamelessly let his eyes fall to the thin clothing that I was sporting, I decided that he was probably as much as an ass as Romeo was. "You look freezing, would you like my coat?" Surprised, I simmered down but before I could answer he was already taking it off, with only a thin wife-beater left under it.

"That's very nice of you, thanks Hidalgo." I smiled at him already feeling warm from his coat but knew that it also involved his kind gesture. "And I would love for you to walk me home," I smirked, "Just as long as you're not, Romeo." I smiled at him and looked back at Romeo and the others, who all had their mouths open and were gawking at the two of us in awe. I gave them a funny look and we started walking.

# Chapter 9

"Don't listen to Romeo, he can be a pompous ass sometimes," he gave me a toothy grin and I smiled at his very thick Cuban accent. We walked along the sidewalk and spoke about our families and friends, thankfully the rain stopped.

"So, I mean, what was that? That dancing was amazing, I just didn't think that Romeo was the person who would be interested in learning that kind of stuff." I laughed and paid attention to him and his baggy clothes, looking at every particular detail. He had what seemed like only a tank top and khaki pants on which I didn't get considering how cold it was, but of course this is coming from the girl who picked skimpy lingerie to go outside in.

"Dancing, what else?" He chuckled. He had a sway in his step like he had nothing else to do but walk and talk with me. I saw so much more in him then a dancer. I saw a care taker, a loner, someone like me.

"Well it was amazing looking, I wish I could learn it, it fascinates me greatly." I grinned, elated. We were at my house, and they sky was a mixture of oranges, pinks, purples and yellows, while the trees were green and brown. "This is my house, I guess I have to go, thanks for walking me home." I politely handed him his tattered brown coat. "Well it was nice meeting you, Hidalgo." I turned to walk away but was stopped by a hot tan hand grabbing my forearm.

"You want to learn? Really?" He locked eyes with me and the eagerness in his voice was intense.

"Yeah, I kinda do," I raise my eyebrows and bit my lip, "Would you like to teach me sometime?"

"I saw you the other day, you can probably dance well, I would like to, yes," He smiled at me making me feel warm from my nose to my toes.

"Well then it's a date, I have the rest of the week off for vacation, so maybe you could stop by sometime, if it's okay with you?" Feeling content around him, I sighed.

"Don't worry, *chica*, that will happen sometime soon," He nodded at me and spun around to walk away, only to have me met by his smile three more times before his body faded into the sunrise.

# Chapter 10

I sauntered inside the door and looked at the clock on my stove, which stated that it was 7:48. My mother didn't seem to be awake- either that or she was hiding from me, because of the big fight we got in last night. I stepped in the guest room, where I would be staying for the time being until I got back on my feet and back to my usual dorm. This used to be my bedroom, and since my mom wasn't into things like repainting-she left the blue paint remain. I still remember that little tear in the wood on the shelf in the closet from when I tried to hide a pocket knife I found from my mom and it nicked the wood. I lightly jogged to the closet after closing my door softly so that I wouldn't wake her.

I looked in the full body mirror to see how bad it was. It looked like I painted the dress on it was so stuck to my body; I peeled it off with frustration. No wonder he was so nice- he probably thought that I dress like this every day. I still wonder why a man who has a million piercings and has the wardrobe of a punk would want to speak Spanish and learn how to dance salsa. Now *that*...that was weird. I couldn't stop thinking about their dancing, though I don't think that I would exactly want to learn that specific choreography.

I put on some jeans, a cotton t-shirt, threw my wet hair up in a pony-tail and plucked a cap from the floor and put it on top of my head before I quietly tiptoed my way into her room to get my wallet.

I changed into a different pair of flats and tossed the others into the dirty clothes basket that was next to my door before I completely made my way out of the guest room. I cracked her door open and then checked to see if she was awake at all before I went in.

She was lazily sprawled on her bed, her blankets around her in a tousle. I quietly sneaked in, and slowly walked over to her bedside. It seemed she never took her dress off and the long fabric draped from the end of her bed. She had a bottle in her hand and about twelve tiny empty bottles on her bed blankets. I slowly took the big bottle out of her hand and read the label, "Smirnoff Liquor". I plucked all the tiny bottles out of her bed comforter and found about six more little bottles under her sheets. She never noticed I was there- It was almost as if she wasn't aware of me moving around her, moving her body over. But...wait...

I shook her shoulders, whispering at her, "Mom? Wake up, Mom- wake up," I shook her harder; her face was down on the pillow so I couldn't see. I slowly pulled her head up and saw foam coming out of her mouth, I looked at her nightstand again and saw acid tablets. I felt a bloodcurdling scream erupt from my throat and I ran to the living room to get the home phone. I called an ambulance, then fell to her bedside crying, yelling at her to wake up. That's when I noticed the note in the bottle that came out of her hand. I smashed it on the floor and didn't care when the tiny little shards splintered into my arms as grabbed the note. "Its your turn. I love you. Mom."

I started hearing police sirens and then the slamming of peoples doors, and people shouting to their neighbors to come outside and see what was going on.

The paramedics rushed into my house, heard my cries and then then flipped my mother over so that they could see the front of her body, I just screamed louder, clutching her hand and strangling the note in my other hand.

"You need to leave, now." They started to pull me away but I just shouted and screamed, yanking away from their grips.

"No! I can't just leave her- *please! Mom, wake up!*" I was whimpering and crying, left over makeup smearing all over my face, mascara streaming. I felt like I was going to be sick and I saw that I was shaking. This wasn't happening, I can't lose her now- I can't lose her ever. I wouldn't go on.

"Get her out of here, now." A strong woman clawed me off of my mother, kicking and screaming.

"Let me go- I can't leave her! Let me go!" I was crying hot tears and watched down the hall as they checked her pulse and immediately put her on the gurney and rushed her out into the ambulance. They let me go and I ran out the front door and into the crowd. I ran to the first person I saw and started crying into their neck and embrace.

"*lo sucedido,* Scarlett*?!*" He immediately put his arms around me and was very, very warm. "What happened, Scarlett?!" He spoke in English and hugged me tight. When I didn't answer he just shushed me and stood there, hugging me as I refused to look at the scene that was going on behind me. "I am so sorry, Scarlett." He rested his chin on top of my head and let out a labored sigh.

"She took something with alcohol. I-I...Mom!" I started crying again, and clamped my eyes shut and only focused on the sound of his heart beat. He was always very warm.

"What happened?" I heard Romeo whisper to him. I caught an angry titch to the somberness in his voice.

Hidalgo's accent immediately adapted to the Spanish, "*Algo pasó con mamá Scarlett's, por lo que Scarlett está muy asustada.*" He turned his head around and looked at Romeo. Hidalgo sighed and I could hear the concern in his voice when he was speaking Spanish to him. "*Ella ha estado llorando durante mucho tiempo, no sé qué hacer al respecto.*" He sighed again in a tone of desperation, and upset. He just stood there desperately staring at Romeo for answers while still hugging me.

"*Es malo? La madre de* Scarlett *va a estar bien, verdad?*" The hardness that come in Romeo's voice shocked me a little bit. Even though I couldn't understand a word that they were saying I knew that they were talking about me and my mother- as bad as a grade I got, I still got some of the basics when I took Spanish.

"*No sé,* Romeo.*" Hidalgo looked back down at me and my ridiculously red hair, still wet from earlier. At least he didn't care that I was hugging him, I don't think that I could have let go, and if I did I would fall to the floor and curl up in a ball.

"*Quédate con ella,* Hidalgo.*" Romeo then disappeared into the crowd, toward the ambulance.

"I don't like it when I can't tell what you are saying." I was hiccupping in between words. I realized that I was crying in this man's shirt and I barely knew him, "I am so sorry, I barely know you and I am already making you all wet with my tears." I pulled away from him and wiped my face, mascara smearing black all over my hands.

"Your mama just got put into an ambulance, you were crying and looked like you needed someone. You had a good reason to make me all wet with your tears, Scarlett." He gave me his best concerned look, "And I didn't mind anyway, *chica.*" He gave me a somber look, with a hint of a smile pulling at his lips.

"Do you think that I am a bad person, Hidalgo?" I felt the hot tears start to run down my face again and I closed my eyes and then imagined last night, how she frowned at me, when she was only trying to do something nice for me. She did so much for me and all I did was scream at her and slam the door in her face. I am the most horrible person in life. I am the most horrible daughter in life.

"No, you are not." He came closer to me and he made me look up at him. "People make mistakes, that is the whole point of life, learning- whether it is learned the hard way or the easy way, we don't know, but that's just how it works." he shook his head at me. "There is no such thing as bad or good, just upset or misunderstood." He put his hands on my shoulders, "Do you want to go with your mama in the ambulance?" he looked down at me with a sad face, his voice barely a hushed whisper.

"Right now, I just need a hug." I started to cry and hiccup again and he gave me a big bear hug to make me feel better. "Do you have a car?" I pulled back again and looked up at him and his worried expression.

"Yes, would you like me to drive you?"

"Yes, please. I can't stand to drive in my mother's car right now." I smeared black all over my arms by drying my eyes again.

"Nina, I left my car at home can I take yours? I'm taking her to the hospital to see her Mama," he turned around to find Nina stand a couple yards away, still in her white shorts and t-shirt, leaning against a tree that was in my front yard, muttering to herself with her eyes wide looking at the scene and finally taking it in.

"Sure, is she going to be okay?" She was speaking in English, she didn't have a Cuban or Mexican accent at all, hers was American. She threw him the keys, a high throw that I could have never caught.

"I don't know." He caught them in a swift motion, flicking his wrist up and down like he was throwing a stone. The way she said it, I don't know if she was talking about me or my mother. Romeo came running up to us, out of breath.

"She is going to be headed to Carmen Hospital. Are you driving her there Hidalgo?" he shot an intense look at Hidalgo, I could almost feel the static that hung in the air between them two. Romeo put a cold hand on my shoulder "Are you going to be okay?"

"Not really. Do you know the way the the hospital, Hidalgo?" I peered back at him, with tears filling my eyes, trying to hold them all back. Trying keep what's left of my dignity still intact.

"*Si, chica*" He skimmed the road for the car and put his gaze upon a brown, beat up car.

You have got to be kidding me.

# Chapter 11

"Lets go." he clasped my hand and then with warm shocks going up and down my arms from the concerned touch coming from his hand, he started to lead me to the car. Even when I was in my worst state, I couldn't help but feel something warm every time I saw him, he was like my personal sun, even in this frigid weather. I got the opposite reaction from Romeo, it was cold chills that went down my spine, but I couldn't tell if they were good or bad. No- they had to be bad.

He was walking quickly with me, tripping on his pants as the ambulance loaded my mom and started to pull out of the ice covered cemented driveway. The van was struggling to get out with the whole crowd blocking the opening of the drive way. The police were shoving worried neighbors and curious street dwellers back, yelling at them to get out of the way and other unpleasant things but I didn't want to think about that- the only thing that I was freaking out about was the fact that she was probably in that ambulance because of me.

They finally got pulled out of the drive then, slightly sliding on the ice doing so. I threw my body into the car, shaking the piece of crap to death. I looked in Nina's way and she shot me a nervous, edgy look that meant "Don't hurt my car, dammit." but also meant "I so can't yell at you because your moms in an ambulance right now."

I just shook her off as Hidalgo whipped the driver's side car door open, it creating an identical dent to the rest on the Mazda Protege, and dived into the car seat, making a puff of dust fly up. He then put his seat belt on and then shut the door with thud. His dark brown hair was flicking back and forth here and there whenever he moved, the hair length to the bottom of his ears. When he started to drive, his hand put the gear into drive and we started following the ambulance on the way to Carmen Hospital.

I was noticed his face, tanned just right, big, dark eyes, slender not a lot of muscle but enough, no blemishes to his face- he was a pretty person.

"What are you staring at, Scarlett?" He gave me a tiny grin, still looking sad, "What? Do I have a hair out of place or something?" Then he turned to the mirror and made a big deal about fixing his hair, looking on both of the sides of his head just to make sure that he made it look believable. I smiled and giggled at him, then felt guilty and regretted that I did. I shouldn't be anything close to laughing right now.

"No, you are just really nice, you know that?" I slightly smiled at him but it didn't reach my eyes. I looked at him and his growing glad expression. I pulled my hair over my shoulder and squeezed it out without knowing that it still had a large about of water in it and a big stream of water ran down the front of my white cotton t-shirt, the middle of it shirt turning practically invisible and showing my bright blue bra and all the black lace that lined it too. "Shit." I let my head fall and I stretched out my shirt from the bottom to see how bad it was. It was spreading to the rest of my shirt.

What do I do now?

"Why did you say-?" He turned to look at me and saw my shirt.

"*Oh.*" He looked around the car and the back seat. Nothing. "Uh.....*mierda!*" he even checked the glove box even. Just registration papers. I just sat there nervously. I looked down again and it was almost as if I had *no* shirt on anymore because it had spread to the rest of my shirt. Next thing I knew he ripped off his wife-beater shirt and handed it to me. I glanced at him doubtfully, raising my eye brows at him. "What? It's all

25

I had to cover you, or you would become a tasteless human Popsicle!" He looked away from me and at the road, averting his eyes politely for me.

"Yes, but *you* will become one, Hidalgo, if you give me your shirt." I scoffed at him, and gestured toward his bare, muscular body, then caught myself staring, and tried to look away and out the windshield window, but then found myself looking back at him anyway. He unfortunately caught me after the fifth look.

He grinned at me and then rolled his eyes at me, the blackish brown irises reflecting off the white of the snow and the brown and blue ice outside. "Do you really think I care?" He held the shirt out to me further, urging me to take it, while keeping one hand on the leather and fur steering wheel. When I didn't take it from him, he sighed and put his wife-beater shirt back on. "You are going to be a royal pain to dance with," He chuckled under his breath and looked ahead with a relaxed grin on his face.

"*Excuse me?*" I turned to glare at him but whipped my hair in his direction causing water to sprinkle on his face.

"Uh, thanks?" He bellowed out a laugh, and dried the rest of his face with the rest of his shirt, not only making is shirt wet but letting me realize how fast the shirt spread to water with even at the tiniest of drops.

"I am so sorry!" I scoot closer to him and checked his face for any water, my face closely inspecting his eyes and the rest of his features. I could feel the hot pressure that dilated in the air that hung between us, the way he was staring deep into my eyes made me get patches of sweat on my neck. "I, uh, think your all good, no water." I sat there leaned in, looking at his face, only inches away from where it would start to push the limits of personal space. "You have pretty eyes." I was looking at all of his face but felt myself looking at one particular part way too much.

He looked up in thought and then raised one one dark eye brow at me, "If I have such pretty eyes then why do you keep looking at my *labios* instead?" He peered at me over his big brown eye brows.

"Uh, what?" I shook my head, confused.

He giggled at me slightly, amused at my weird expression. He leaned in closer focused on my lips. "*Labios*, lips, *chica*, lips." he was looking down at mine, then had a sly smile on his face and looked back up at me, entertained and questioning.

"They are pretty too." I looking down at my shirt again and then snapped back to normal, before anything happened. I barely knew him. "Now..." I pulled back and sighed in frustration, "Give me the damn shirt." I raised a plucked brow at him, playful.

His sneaky smile vanished, then he grinned sideways at me, and sighed in defeat. "As you wish," then backed up and away from our earlier stance. I sat back in my seat and lounged, letting all my muscles unclench for a moment, at least trying to relax through everything that was going on. "Here. Plus, *chica,* I am not that easy to be dazzled." He grinned back at me and shook his head - not even affected by the stabbing glare I retaliated with.

26

# Chapter 12

We took the exit off of interstate 90, heading toward the hospital- me worried half to death, Hidalgo driving like a flipping maniac because I ordered him too, and all the meanwhile everything was running through my mind so fast like those people who talk in the auctions that my Aunt Lydian used to take me too when I was five.

I had flashbacks of the fight skimming over and over in my head like I was spinning, like I was falling. All the reports were ringing over and over the same thing repeating- echoing all around me as I heard all the words my mother said to me all my life, saying to be strong, I will be okay, I'm her little trooper, shes so proud of me; you can do it, your my rock, you would never give up on me, I love you honey, that's my Scarlett, Hun I would never stop loving you, don't be scared, you are always smart enough, you lovely little thing, Be happy- my life is too short to see you sad...

All of this was bringing me to tears, letting me think of all the hugs, kisses and nurtures shes given me- never letting me go, never letting me quit or kid myself. I remember the time when I almost told her about dad.

"Darling, what is the use of tears? We have enough water in the fridge! Whatever it is, is not worth spending time being sad and wasting valuable time that could be spent being happy. Tell your mama this big issue that you are having..." I watched the old scene play in my head, with the tears rolling down my face and the little girl's face in the home video playing in my mind.

"I fell, and hit my knee!" I whined at her clutching my little knee cap and rolling on the black, plaid couch back and forth, digging my face in the fabric, hiding my feelings and tears, letting the overwhelming smell of smoke linger in my lungs as I sniffed the scratchy-soft cushion. I coughed into the couch but wouldn't move from the crack of the cushion and the floor, not showing my eyes and the red rings that hung under them from shock and fear, reluctantly breathing it in, gagging a little more.

"Well let me see, come on, Scarlett- let me see it," Her soft, plush hands scrolled over the skin by the big gash on my knee, letting my hand give for her to feel around it; somehow wishing to make everything better again. She gasped and rubbed my shoulder in comfort, clearly worried about me, "Scarlett, how did this happen? It seems a little worse than a tiny cut." I could feel my hot hands sticky with my blood, shake in desperate anxiety, searching my head for an answer, feeling the grainy blood drips run down in my leg slowly, creating a painful itch that I so much wanted to scratch.

"I fell, mom." I squeezed my eyes together, and kept poking at my pointer finger with my thumbnail, tapping back and forth, starting to stab deeper and deeper into the crimson covered index finger. I slowly pushed my face and torso into the crack, letting me sink in- letting the guilt take over thinking how the white lie slipped through my lips so quickly and easily. My fists slipped through the crack reluctantly, afraid of some hands that were going to grab my arms and pull me under into the smoky smelling haze, but knowing I still couldn't tell her about myself therapy...my way to cope and keep what was going on a secret. She has noticed the scars and all the bruises forming on my head from falling, tripping and then banging my head on the furniture, or at least those were my excuses for a cover up of what was really going on.

There was a long pause and I could sense her rigid posture growing as my silence grew, the more I was quiet, the more I sunk into the couch. I felt myself being pulled under and I started to whimper. "You fell or you were pushed. Scarlett Elena Todd, don't lie to me." Her tone was sharp and I could feel her narrowed eyes jabbing my back, making me more nervous. I yanked myself out of the crack, my blood covered hands now white with fuzz. I felt my eyes grow wide and then felt a scream pushing at my throat, but I shoved it down and started picking it off, but not getting it off fast enough.

"Mom- help me get it off." Ripping it off, I whispered to her, waving my hands in front of her for her to help, a confused face overcame her expression and then she started to quickly prick it off of my hands, avoiding my own fingers that were ripping and flicking at it. Once I got it all off of my hands I continued to breathe hard.

"Scarlett, what are you not telling me?" She had shock and mere fear for me painted on her face. She reached out to hug me and take me in her arms but I knew that if she did, I would have felt safe and then told her, and then I would be in trouble with Daddy. I moved away from her and headed off toward the bathroom, feeling like sleeping but went to the bathroom to avoid her touch and everyone else's.

"I fell." Then I shut the door behind me and locked it- hearing it make a tiny click, then I heard footsteps come into the hall- big heavy boots. He came in from sitting on the porch. I ran the bath, as much hot water as possible, thinking of the theory of boiling myself to death, then a slight knock on the door sounded make a shiver ripple through me. I sat on the cold green and yellow tiled floor cross-legged in my sunflower dress, which was yellow all over, and stared at the door, watching the shadows of two feet cast on the bottom, the white sunlight trailing around them as they moved closer and further around the whereabouts of the door.

"Scarlett?" he called in to me, with the normal curiosity that carried in his voice that always frightened me. I sat there staring at the door my eyes widening and watering at the slow turning of the doorknob and then the sound of the car leaving the driveway, mom honking the horn twice like she always does- signaling that she was leaving. I closed my eyes silently begging her not to leave. When I opened them I found the doorknob had stopped turning. "I'm coming in, Scarlett." his gruff voice becoming impatient with me, his breath quickening with repulsive excitement as he starts to get the lock. I stand up and walk towards the toilet and let my body squeeze between the space between the toilet and the sink that had a cabinet covered space- hiding my body as quietly and quickly as possible. I had myself slide in and then quieted my breathing, the space I was hiding in completely quiet except for the water that was running in the green bathtub. The door opened wide and I didn't move, my body grew tense.

He glanced around the bathroom and then stepped toward the bathtub, crouched down and shut the water off, which I knew that the tub was barely full and it was just a way for him to listen. I slowly pushed myself slowly inward, moving more close in hiding, scared of what would happen if he found me, wondering what he would make me do this time. I tapped the switch on the toilet once accidentally, sounding a tiny metallic *clink*. His head shot up and his eyes traveled to the toilet and then unexpectedly he stood up, walked out of the bathroom and closed the door behind him. I sat there and slowly let out a breath while I listened to him close the front door with a slam, signaling that he left.

I slipped out of the crack and then turned the bath back on, locking the door and but put a chair under it this time, and started to strip off the bubbly yellow sunflower dress and tights. I finally got my underwear off when I heard footsteps quickly walk to the bathroom door, before I had time to even think of what to do- the door was ripped open, he was standing there with a creepy, drunk smile slurred across his face, showing that he had been drinking again. "Want some help, Scarlett?" I felt myself shake my head for the answer no, but before I knew it he slipped into the bathroom, clicked at door shut behind him, locked it- sticking the chair under the doorknob and then walked over to me and started grazing his hands over my shoulders.

"No! Don't!" I screamed and lunged in front of me to smack my father in the face before he could touch me- but I was still in Nina's car, still heading toward the hospital, and Hidalgo was still driving me.

"Scarlett, are you okay?!" His gave me a shaky look and panicked from my freak reaction to nothing. He swerved the car over but then everything was back to being strait on the road faster than he swerved. I was hyperventilating and the inside of the car started to spin. I started wavering back and forth in my seat.

"Just give me a minute to put myself back together." I sat back in my seat and felt a loud heartbeat wrench through all the thoughts in my mind and I felt like I went cross eyed as everything doubled on me, the car turning into the bathroom then back- images of green and yellow spinning and then all of a sudden it would change back to brown and tan, "I think I'm going to be sick!" I doubled over and felt like I was about to puke all over the car when I heard skid marks and a horn honking over and over. Next thing that happened, I sat up and saw that the ambulance was skidding over the end of the bridge from the impact of getting hit by a semi-truck and they were starting to slide into the ice layered river along with the semi-truck, "No!" I shrieked and yanked her car door open while we were still sliding on the ice and hopped out, falling on my face trying to run over to the edge.

But when I looked up, it was already too late.

# Chapter 13

Both fell over the edge, I heard the brain-wracking crack of the ice and then the splash from the vehicles dunking their way down into the water. *"Mom!"*

I struggled to stand up and when I finally got the chance, I ran towards the edge, slipping, and heaved my chest over the railing, hoping that they just landed on the ice with a thud and were alive, but reality came crashing down when I saw the gaping hole inside of the ice and the ambulance and semi-truck were nowhere in sight.

"Mom, no!" I screeched into the air. I could feel myself slipping and falling over the edge as I reached toward the black water. I saw as my tears fell from the altitude of the icy bridge and then froze in mid air falling halfway to the ice of the river. I ached out a bloodcurdling roar and then my body tumbled over the edge. I hollered and grabbed the ledge with both hands dangling from the frigid bridge.

"Scarlett hold on!" I looked over the street to find Hidalgo sprinting towards the edge, tears running from the cold air that was pulling him back when it started to snow. It felt like the sky turned black and burning blue flakes started to pour over on the whole scene as if saying its own goodbyes. My fingers started to slip then I was just dangling from one arm instead of two, my fingers on the one hand that was holding on slipping-palms and fingers burning like someone caught them in an ice fire, persisting them to let go.

I started to wail and then let go and began to free fall towards the river, thinking that I would soon be joining my mom, but before I got three feet from the ledge Hidalgo grabbed me with a hot hand and yanked me back up yelling for me to hold on and not let go. He struggled as I tried to stay as relaxed and quick as possible, pulling myself up, with my arms muscles screaming.

He yanked me up and hugged my shivering body, desperately trying to make me stop chattering and get warm. I started whimpering in his chest, and watched at the flakes fell on his tan skin and evaporated so quickly. They couldn't last on his scorching body temperature. I cried and I cried knowing that I could never take back what I said and what was done is done. She is gone- it's over. I'm over. I can't do anything now but cry.

# Chapter 14

The helicopters were everywhere, people were swarming, it was like the aftermath of an earthquake. Everyone was either crying or on their toes wondering who perished, and what exactly happened. I sat there, right in front of that bridge where the railing was ripped from the pavement, right where my mother fell with the others. I wouldn't leave the spot that I was sitting in no matter who tried to make me move. I just sat there and waited to see my mother come climb up the side of the bridge and tell me everything was going to be okay and that she was okay. I was tuned everyone out; teachers, students, neighbors, friends, family, reporters, police- everyone was trying to get through to me...but I refused to even look at them.

Since I would not speak, Hidalgo did all the explaining, telling them everything including that my mother was in the ambulance. The black ice was left untouched by anyone who was in that ambulance, but the waiting didn't feel pointless in my heart. In my heart, I knew that she was alive, someone would have found her and when I closed my eyes- this would all just be some scary nightmare and when I would wake up, Mom would greet me in the morning with breakfast and again changing the arrangement of all the spice jars, and I would apologize and forget about all this mess. The wishful thinking was my only way to cope with the fact that my mother might be gone forever.

"Ma'am, we need to get you to the hospital to check your health. You might have gotten frost bite from sitting on the ice. Ma'am?" The man that was trying to speak to me had an Indian accent and was speaking in a stutter from the weather, but I wasn't cold...I felt hot actually. Really, really hot. A blurred figure came in my sight range, upon my teared eyes. He was a big tan blob, with big black spots for eyes and a blurred black and blue suit or clothing of some sort. I just starred on, patiently waiting for her to come.

A tall, slender, handsome boy about my age stepped in front of him and bent down in front of me to look at my face. Everything else was blurred but that one boy sat there, squatted down- looking deeply into both my eyes, showing the reflection of my mother in them making me reach for him slightly. His body was the only thing that wasn't blurred from my tears, it was almost as if the world around him was fading and it was just him, squatting there, staring into my eyes as I reached out for him slowly. He moved back hesitantly then stared at my hand as if questioning 'why'. His voice was so silky it made me think that his voice box was made of chocolate a cream. "Would you like to say goodbye to your mother?" He looked at me like I was fragile, trying his best to stay gentle with me.

I looked down at my hands, which were red and shaking, very dry but moisturized with the cold seasonal air, telling me to get help. I peered up at the boy a little, admiring his angelic glow that made tears run. His blond hair was a little ratted but in a styled way so that it seemed that way on purpose, his one dimple sending a sad smile my way, giving me an inviting tone in his voice, not one like I needed help. I gave the slightest movement of my eyes, and a twitch of my head that was trying to give him the impression of a nod.

"I don't want to say goodbye, though- I don't want her to go." I whispered so faintly it was barely a breath. He raised his brow slightly and then sighed at me.

"You may not have both worlds, Scarlett- because it's inevitable." He then stood up strait again and made his way over the edge and leaned down for to Scarlett's surprise a white hand grabbed it and she watched the miracle happen through her own eyes. He pulled her mother up, her purple dress sticking to her body, her tresses drenches.

I stood strait up knocking someone who was in front of me over, and I could hear a bunch of bones crack in my legs as I strained to move my limbs, while other parts of my body was suffering severe burning pains and sensations.

I walked over and stood there, starting to hiccup over and over, somehow through it all hearing myself choke out "I love you mom, don't go." I started to whisper to her and heard myself pleading over and over for her not to go, not to die, not to leave me, not to suffer, not to regret, not to be sad, and most of all not to forgive me for the way I treated her over my life.

She just stood there and shook her head at me then smiled, "Honey, you don't understand," she giggled at me in joy, "I am *free* now, everything happens for a reason, and that is why I am going, because it is *your* time to live out your life and figure some things out." she came closer to me carrying a drift with every movement she made,

"You need to know the secret that he has been hiding,
Remember the times when your father and I were fighting,
And he just wouldn't listen to me- he just wouldn't care,
Well here's a task that no one would dare.
You father never told me what he used to do,
What he used to do that was so vile to you,
I didn't figure it out until recently then,
That he used to molest you in the den,
I am so sorry, Scarlett, I never knew,
The horrible things he was doing to you,
But your father is nowhere to be found,
And that's where it comes in the tight bound,
That you must make- that you must choose,
If you do this for me no one will lose,
The game he is playing- you will win,
He has a dark secret that he hasn't even told kin,
You need to find this out- where he is hiding,
Because there are other girls out there like you that are trying,
Not to get taken away from predators like your dad,
I tried looking for it but it just made me really mad,
Because I couldn't find what he was hiding at all,
What lies behind his sick dirty wall?
Of secrets and lies and hate and betrayal,
I tried and I tried but what I only did was fail,
So I need you to do this for me- or do it for those kids,
I have no idea where he went or what he did,
That made him drop from the earth so easily and quick,
And here's where comes in the little trick,
I need you to find him- to see what he did,
What he's hiding that could be so morbid,
But be careful my dear- because he can be dangerous,
Hopefully the sorrow he makes isn't contagious...
But do this for me, Scarlett- do this for them,
And know that I love you now, forever, and then."

She was speaking in rhyme and I went over it over and over in my head. So, she knew about dad? Since when?

"Yes, Hun, I did, I put the pieces together. Baby, I am so sorry that I didn't know till just now." She came over and kissed my cheek, a powerful wind blew in my face, in response to it. "It's your turn to look for his secret- the one I have been searching for, for so long." She then turned toward the ledge and walked up to it, then tilted her head back to look at me, "You never did anything wrong to make me disappointed in you, so quit worrying that you did something to make that happen." She giggled and grabbed on to an old man that just appeared standing there.

"Grandpa?" I whispered in awe at him, shaking my head a little not believing that I am actually meeting him.

"That Great Grandpa to you little miss!" he chuckled and I looked back at mom, who was now a little girl in a nightgown, holding a tall, muscular man's hand. Mom in her little gown and holding her tattered teddy bear looked back at me and waved and yelled in a young voice that sounded much like mine when I was little, "Bye Scarlett!" She giggled again and they walked off the ledge.

# Chapter 15

"I need a heart pump, *Now!*" I heard a man yell at someone; my vision was wavering, and my hearing was bleeping in and out. I felt myself on some hard fabric, and it smelled like medication, urine, and fresh plastic in this place. There was a vibration coming from out and under me, and the sound of murmuring and the hard slapping of shoes rang in my ears. I couldn't feel any part of my body besides my hands and my head. I saw white everywhere and the room was spiraling and moving all over the place, giving me a raging migraine.

"What's wrong?! Why can't we see her? What's going on?" I could hear Ivy and Sarah's cries from down the hallway. Then I felt myself giving in to the feeling of nausea and letting go into the blackness that was aching so badly to put me into slumber.

"Dr. Ishmael, we don't have much time, if you don't do it now she will be gone- do it, *Now!*" The vibration that was under me came to a stop and the last thing I could hear was static, and a screaming of a mob down the hall. The last thing that I thought about was that boy on the bridge...

His glow that radiated from his being was eye opening and I could almost swear that I have seen him before. Was this what it felt like to have a flashback? I could almost remember the hard marble of his skin, when he came through my front door with a big crooked smile on his face, wearing his overalls...but I didn't exactly know *if* I really knew who he was. I fell into a big dark dream after that, after hearing the strange people outside me and my vibrating body.

I was in a field, and I could sense that he was there with me too. The field was so beauteous that I couldn't catch my breath correctly. I had a field of red daisies all around me as the twilight twinkled above.

With night coming, the moon started to sprout, and even though the sun would have been bright, the new-found moon seemed to blind me with how big it was and how luminous it was. If that thing were a flat circle and fell out of the sky, it could crush the earth it seemed. I felt like I was in a creepy book where the feeling of being watched starts to slide in my brain. The girl in the field, all alone...probably is pretty and good to kidnap.

The moon not only makes the night more radiant looking...but the flowers somehow look darker, like their color deepened and got richer. I sat there, staring at everything around me, thinking what this was all about. I was sitting in the only plain ground in miles it felt and seemed like, but this spot had two butt and four shoe prints and it was big enough for someone else to sit down, cross-legged along with me.

It looked like a nightmare but I was content as if it was a relaxing dream. I glanced down and realized that I was wearing a white dress. It was studded with red rhinestones though, right where the cleavage was entirely exposed and looked like everything just started to *spill* out, like an adult lying in an overfilled bathtub. I pulled it up in an effort to cover myself better but it was no use. I could tell who ever was smart enough in this dream to make the top a *tiny bit* smaller than I needed, was most likely male. It had embroidered red glitter tracing the ends of the dress, where it fell at the bottom, and where the straps on top fell a little bulky.

I pondered on the scenery for a little bit longer. There were fireflies everywhere, illuminating *every* flower in the field. It was beautiful in an uncomfortable way though. I felt like a princess and a future murder victim at the same time- it was complicated. The scenery was unreal, but the air smelled of death and strange cologne. Then I saw a figure in the distance- they were tall, I could tell that much at least. The man, (I could tell from the bulky structure on their body), was surrounded by a bunch of stacked rectangular figures, and his hair was short and spiked, shining silver in the blinding moonlight.

The man turned to me, his bright gray eyes enticing me to start walking. I stood and my exuberant white glittered heels started to slightly sink in the dirt as I made my way over, a path of daisies cleared, and my mind seemed to only be seeing a swirling picture of optical illusion.

Once I snapped out of it I was standing in front of the man and he towered over me, his wings glowing iridescent black. He stared me down with a look of concentrated sadness, his chest bare, and his black sweat pants looked almost like they were made out of smoke or air, that was how light they seemed on him. He stepped toward a stack of books and handed one to me, it was blue leather with a peacock feathers in it like the feathers were a part of the skin. I looked on the cover, and on it in gold script it said this: *"Look upon the pages."* I shuddered at the mere chill that vibrated around the book. There was only one problem that stirred angrily in my mind. It had a lock.

I peered up and moved my lips to speak, but nothing came out of them. Then a light blasted into my mind and blinded my head of all other thoughts, the pressure on my head was excruciating. A beautiful voice of silk spoke to me saying words but not moving his lips.

"These are the only words that may come out,
You can try in this place but can never scream about,
Speaking is forbidden for ones who come,
It's actually forbidden for anyone,
So here is a word that you need to know,
You make the rules and call the show,
But here the only thing that the seeker dreads,
Is broken hearts and tears that shed."

I saw the somberness in his eyes that held tears, but the tears he held would not come out. He held them in with all of his might and managed to suck it up.

I pointed at the lock and made a look of question at his beautiful face. He pointed at my neck line and smiled again sadly at the half-broken heart on the golden chain that hung around my neck. I remember this necklace...My dad, Sebastian gave it to me on my third birthday and I hated him so much, that I hid it and never put it on. There on the lock was a ragged little hill that had sharp cuts that seemed to match my side of the broken heart.

He motioned with his hands for me to take the necklace off and then stick it in the lock. I unscrewed the back and pulled it off my bony upper torso, and pressed it into the lock. The book sprung open in my hands, ripping the cover open and somehow burning my palms and fingers. I dropped it and clutched my hands, a silent howl letting out from my throat.

He snatched it off the ground and started flipping through it, and then he spoke aloud. What the hell?

*"Yes, finally!"* He then noticed that I was staring, "Do you know how long I haven't spoke? God, thank you!" then he ran over and crushed me in a bear hug, his muscular

arms squeezing me to a pulp, lifting be about five feet off the ground until I saw that we were levitating, and he was flying. I felt the panic come rushing into me.

I started to spit words at him, but nothing came out, as I tried to tell him to let me down, that I had freaked fear of heights ever since I was little. I squirmed and I flung trying to break free.

"Okay, okay, I get it- you don't like hugs! *Jeez!*" He put me down and chuckled at me like he just got away with stealing a cookie from the jar without getting caught.

I was still mad, how could he forget about me? I jerked my hand towards my mouth and pointed, talking soundless. He raised his brow and then jumped up like someone pinched his ass, "Oh! I almost forgot!" He grabbed my hand, with me still talking at him, and poked the middle of my palm so hard that I screamed without noise and just when I started to talk again my voice started working.

"Fuck! What the hell?!" I grabbed my hand and saw that my burn marks from the book started to fade away and the burning sensations in my hand started to go away as well.

"Excuse me, but I was expecting a thank you!" He cocked his head in a way that made him look very silly. "But I should be thanking you I guess- you saved my voice. It's almost like the tale of the Little Mermaid...Ursula takes her voice and then she has to get it back somehow." He smiled softly at me and tucked his arms around his wings.

"I don't know what I did to have you thank me besides opening a book." I gazed up at him, so tall...so *pale*. I was completely healed by now, the air around me was very cool, but everything else besides it is warm to the touch.

The wind blew my hair back and it felt like the great moon was putting its touch effect on me. I stretched my arms out and let the wind take me. The bright red daisies under me and around me started growing rapidly, and I shot up in the sky. When I looked around me, up this high the sky was bright pink, and the horizon was peaking. Down there it was dark, and the moonlight shined sadness and sleepiness. Up here you felt free...like you were flying. The wind was perfect, and strong against my shoulders to my fingertips, and any other part of my body.

I put my arms up in the air. Flower petals from the east of me rose off of their flowers and blew my way. Once they came, they kissed against my skin and they swirled around me. The wind swirled in a whirlwind around me and pulled my hair, which miraculously grew longer, up and pulled it to its longest length, the flower petals now intertwining in my hair, making little barrettes throughout all of it.

I watched up and ogled when I saw my hair stretched about six feet long and was a bright black. The red barrettes melted inside my hair dying it a bright purplish-red again, and then just like that, most of my hair fell off and was short. My hair fell into the abyss under the red daisies. I didn't feel as free anymore without the long hair for some weird reason, and with the black in my hair, I looked so...*tan*. I was surprised though, because usually I never tanned, I always sun burned.

He floated over to me slowly- as if with caution. His expression squinted slightly at the approaching yellow ball, his face practically glowing gold in the flickering lighting of the quivering sunset. He had his hands stuffed in his pockets and his structure looked rigid, but relaxed on the toned skin.

"Your hair was like that in a past life. I remember how you looked on that day I first met you." He was inspecting the sunset like he was before, as if all those memories lay right there on the suns surface. He sat down on the powdery, pollinated ground and his face was twisted, deep in thought. His black wings arched around his arms from habit, and his body still seemed oh-so white, even in this gold lighting.

"You were in the back of a dirty brown pick-up truck, your long, long black hair tumbled in big waves of luscious waterfalls over your shoulders and down your back- so long that you were sitting on it with your legs crouched, bent over a stack of books that all read *Shakespeare* on the spines.

"You were in the middle of reading *Othello,* and then you put it down and picked up the most atrociously warred book. It had pages that were burned on the edges, pages sticking out, drawings shoved in. You ran your long, nail-less fingers over and over the blue leather cover, tears running down your cheeks. Your hair shone so silky and bright in the hot sunlight, your face was dirty and your clothing was slightly in tatters. It was in the late time when men could have multiple wives and agriculture was rich in the air with trade. I worked at the local market as a trader and your truck pulled up. Before a man came out of the car, you quickly put all the books away in a tarp, including the warred one and wiped your tears and pulled yourself together before he could notice anything.

"Then a man who rose tall and high above me stepped out of the car and slammed the door shut. His brown hair was greasy and tousled on his head. He had a mean expression fixed there and was chewing on a piece of straw. He snapped his fingers and called you out of the back, you just hopped up out of the back and went to his side almost like you were his servant. He was buying grain for whatever, and I wanted to ask but I wasn't allowed to socialize with the customers. But that didn't stop me at all from looking at you, from staring at the beautiful potential I knew you had behind all that dirt and grime, just watching you all the time."

He turned his face to mine, with his striking, now silver, eyes holding the story with in them. I could see from the expression on his face that he felt love in this story- he cherished it. He looks so... It's like I *know* him! Which I obviously did in a past life...whatever this all means for him to tell me? I had no idea in my mind of why he was doing all of this explaining, but I had to admit hearing about it was fascinating so I didn't speak. I just kept looking into the sunset and thinking when was it was ever going to set already?

My hair slowly started to grow as he was telling me the story of part of my past. It suddenly became darker and darker, becoming dark purple, then brown, then dark brown, and soon a shimmering silky black. It stretched past my waist and then past my butt. Once it finished growing it went to my mid thigh, and it hovered in a black glittery cape around my shoulders. I ran my fingers through it and it felt as silky as it looked on my back.

"You like it?" I didn't know whether he was talking about the hair or the story, but I nodded anyways still running my fingers through my hair and looking at the ends noticing that it was perfect and had no split ends, it was also cut so strait all around that there were no layers or anything. I did like it- it felt more...me for once, and I haven't even thought of the events that happened earlier before I came here.

"I like it very much," I looked at him with new eyes, noticing a big change. Suddenly he had his hair trimmed a little bit and his hair was blonder now, and he was wearing baggy dark jeans, and a loose black shirt with short sleeves. Now I knew who he was-

"It can't be..." I started to back up and before I could even see his reaction, I ran away from him, and then the flower floor that my heels were padding on opened just a crack and I fell down. Further and further and further I went down, getting darker and darker, until soon I couldn't see the ground at all before I met the wet dirt floor with a crushing force on my body's limbs.

# Chapter 16

I had to catch the breath that just got knocked out of me. It took me twice as long to catch my breath seeming as there was a very big and heavy object on top of me. My eyes shot open to find glasses, black hair, and a tattoo of a dragon and a Chinese sign on a flimsy bicep.

"I landed a lot harder than I should have. Scarlett, what the fuck happened to your hair?!" His voice spoke to me. No- he needs to get the fuck out of my room and now.

My eyes bulged and I stopped breathing for a moment. I didn't want to see anyone, let alone *him.*

"You have five *fucking* seconds to get off my body and out of my room before I punch you so hard in the mouth that you will quickly bleed out." With my eyes closed, my hands clenching in fists, and my teeth grinding together from even seeing him five inches *close* to me, I felt myself starting to lose my sanity and patience- and fast.

"But I only-"

"*Four!*"

"You started on five-"

"*Three!*" I was pretty sure that I was going to lose control and punch him right then.

"Scarlett-"

"*Don't speak to me!*"

"Wait Scarlett-" He was standing now with his hands held above his head in surrender, backing little inches away at a time, edging to the door.

I saw red flowers of some sort in a vase next to me, took the flowers out and chucked the vase at him with a grunt. "*One!*"

He ducked in time and it smashed against the door. He spun around to see the broken crystal and ogled back at me, "What the hell, Scarlett?"

Then two nurses shoved past him and ran to me in panic, while I could hear the heart monitor beeping get faster and faster.

"Sir, you need to leave! Your upsetting the patient and her blood pressure isn't supposed to be high-" Two nurses ran over to my cot and grabbed my arms struggling to pin me down, but I was already halfway off, fast-crawling to the end of my bed to run over to him when they grabbed my arms and started to pull. An African-American lady and a scrawny, pale, blond-haired woman we're fighting at my sides, yanking and scratching on my arm skin.

"We *passed* that rule ages ago!" I got one hand free and reached out to claw him to death, "What the *hell*, is *Shane Kindle* doing here?!" They grabbed my arm in a feeble attempt to hold me back and another nurse came in with a Wake-talkie and pushed a button on their pager, then she turned on the talkie and whispered urgently "We've got a distressed tantrum thrower. I'm going to need security and more nurses." then came over and shoved both of my arms down until I couldn't sit back up. My grunts and screams echoed down the hall and I could hear the footsteps of people come with great speed.

Security came through the door and shoved Shane back out, escorting him out the door. I was screaming for them to get off of me when all of a sudden I felt a hard pinch in my arm and I started to feel drained as my body became really numb.

"I hated to do that sweetie, but you left me no choice." the nurses let me go and I slid down into my bed. The room went all spiny on me then all of a sudden there was a little pan under my chin and the scrawny nurse was making me take a pill with the glass of water. The pan was so locked underneath my chin that I had a hard time swallowing it down.

"We won't let that boy back in your room, Hun. Promise." I about gagged at what she called me.

I saw the flashes run through my mind. Black ice. The bridge. Wet clothing and cold. Frigid, unbearable cold. My mother is dead. No more lunch visits, no more weekend garage sales, no more diner cuts. No more anything. I felt like I couldn't move- which I couldn't have if I tried because of what they gave me. I felt like jelly on the inside.

What was I going to do with myself? She was the only one who really cared about me, like, in a way no one could understand. I wanted to crawl into a ball and melt away into nothing so no one could ever look at me anymore. So no one could see me ever again.

"You know, that was some fit you threw there. You must really hate that boy, what is he? The ex?" The African-American nurse said to me with a pen tip in her mouth, which seemed as if it was about to fall because it could barely holding on for the ride. I was breathing deep in my chest and every word that I tried to say made me completely out of breath.

"Yes...don't...wanna...talk..." I said barely making out the words, as I spoke in a slip. She nodded and held up her hand to tell me silently that she got the point. Finally I felt a little more able to move and speak normally and I slowly sat up inside my medical bed and breathed through the racking pain in my back from sitting hunched over at the bridge.

Looking at my mother's death spot.

Something really soft was brushing against my back. I sat there for a moment breathing in and out raspy breaths, thinking about how my life isn't going to collapse right now and I'm not going to have a break down in the middle of the hospital.

"Oh, here let me help you with that." Then the nurse who paged security, and had big green eyes and blackish brown hair came over and as I dosed off, she started doing something with my head, slightly tugging and pulling and putting pressure. While she did that I saw that someone put the red flowers in a different vase and put fresh water in it too. There was a manila card with hand written words on it. One of the nurses saw me eying it and plucked it out of the bright red flowers of some kind, and handed it to me. I was still a little woozy so the red flowers were just a big mass that I couldn't make out what kind they were.

*Hope you like your new look.*
*-Heth*

Heth? I saw what looked like a pair of glasses next to the vase and put them on, all of a sudden everything was super focused and I could see the pores on the nurse's faces. I felt something on the back of the card; it was powdery substances that come off of the back that was bright red on my fingers. I turned the card to find a written message in red pastels, and read the message out loud.

*P.S. - Oh, and put on the glasses. They will help.*

"Ooh! Who is *that* from?" a peachy, small chested woman, who looked about my age, trailed in with a candy stripper uniform on and a hospital assistant jacket on as well, with her strawberry blond hair and a field of freckles spread on the plains of her face.

She hopped over and bounced on my bed, scoot in, pulling the covers over her legs and tilted her head over to take a peek at my card reading the red print over and over then made me jump when she gasped. "You have a *boyfriend*? God! You know how long I have been wanting a boyfriend? No one wants to date me though, ugh. But anyways *you gotta boyfriend! you gotta boyfriend! La la la la la la!"* She sang into a chorus of taunting phrases, and I didn't know who this girl was and why she was so comfortable with me.

"Bambi! Can you leave the poor girl alone? It's enough she has to spend a week with you, let alone a day! She's tired and uh..." Big green eyes came over and tugged on her arm and pulled her over to the corner of the room and she finished her sentence in a hushed voice that I couldn't hear.

"Oh...okay." She came over and sat on the chair next to my bed instead, feeling the awkward silence growing as I glared at all of them, staring them down. Then she plunged into a mass of questions, throwing them at me from left and right, "Who is he? What's his name? Does he have a car? What does he do? What does he *do*?" She did not just say that. Dear god...

"Does he live close? Are you in love? Is he in love? Did you say you love him yet? Did he? *Give me all the details, I wanna know everything!"* She was on her elbows, head cocked up at me. "Oh and did I mention that you have the most *beautiful* hair have ever *seen*?" She hopped out of her chair and took hold of my ponytail- my *long* ponytail.

My *long black* ponytail.

I grabbed it and screeched at the top of my lungs, "What the fuck happened to my hair?" I yanked on it over and over thinking that somehow it could fall off...which the thought brought déjà vu. "Oh my god! *Oh my god!"* I was beginning to have a panic attack, because that couldn't possibly have happened. This can't happen! This isn't even possible!

"What is wrong with you?! I think their amazing!" she squealed at me, she slid the ponytail out of my hair and ran he fingers through it, taking it all in,"It's so *silky*! I would *kill* to have your hair!" she stood up and stretched it out as far as she could, without yanking. "Vicky, get a measuring tape! Her hair is *long!"* she yelled to the African-American nurse who was supposedly 'Vicky'. Vicky laughed and pulled one out of her pocket, which of course got me thinking 'oh, wow'.

Bambi grabbed the measuring tape and then had Vicky hold the tip of the measuring tape to my roots, and then Bambi stretched it out to the tip of my hair.

"I got it!"

# Chapter 17

Three feet and four inches. That was how long my hair was. Three feet and four inches. How was I going to explain this to anyone? What was I going to say to people? *Oh, yeah- my hair? Oh don't worry about that, one night it just grew about three more feet long or so and dyed itself black! Anyways, so how was that rainstorm last night?* Uh, I choose not.

"Ooh! This is just so awesome! I mean when does this happen to anyone? Oh wait-"

"Yeah, it's never happened to anyone." I said monotonously.

"Oh. Well look at the nice side of things! You have the prettiest hair *I* have ever seen and that's saying something." She beamed at me, cheeks red, her pretty eyes looking at me with such gratitude. She always had something nice to say it seemed, which was good- with everything going on right now, I think I needed some positivity.

"Well...uh, thanks, that's really nice of you. Now what were you talking about staying with me for a week?" Maybe this would be good for me I mean for moral support and everything-

"Oh! Yeah, I almost forgot. I have to stay with you at all times for a whole week to make sure you don't...you know?" Then she turned her back to the nurses to interact cutting her throat with her hands, and then she made an awkward expression at me.

"You're *babysitting* me? Bu-but I don't get it! I'm fine! See?" I gestured toward myself and I could feel the moisture pulling at the ends of my eyes. Bambi came over and put a soft thin hand on my shoulder, and spoke to me softly and carefully.

She hesitated at the right words to say and looked me over as if trying to believe that I really was okay. She grabbed my other hand with her hand tightly, "Honey, your shaking." she held my hand in front of my face and let go, letting it slightly jiggle on its own.

"You may think your fine, but they are just worried about you, I think that you might not only be stuck with me for awhile but that you might need me." She smiles at me gingerly, the thought bringing color to her cheeks, tears ripping through the surface too on her face, and her voice shook while she spoke honestly to me, "I lost my mom too, she died right in front of my eyes and I couldn't do anything about it because I was too little to understand what was going on. She smiled at me that night before and said before bed, '*Dream beautiful things*'. That morning she took a bunch of pills together and started to cough on the couch...then she just lay there while I tried to wake her up." She was hiccupping now, and no one was in the room anymore except us. Bambi patted my shoulder and leaned in and whispered, locking eyes with me, "But I can be there for you, Scarlett. I understand what you're going through." Her eyes were red with tears and black memories, I nodded and felt a tear run down my face too.

"Okay." She then collapsed into me and I hugged her for what seemed like about an hour. Once we pulled ourselves together she helped me check out of the hospital. Once they slipped her some prescription pills for me that I was not allowed to see, and when we hit the lobby I got almost trampled by a crowd of people, but the first ones to ambush me were Sarah and Ivy. They rapped their arms around me and squeezed me tight, to the point to where I wasn't able to breathe.

"Oh my god- your okay!" they both whimpering and sniffling really loud into my shoulders and they squeezed me awhile, just standing there. "We were worried sick about you!" The others politely waited for them to be finished and get their turn, but then grew impatient after a little while. I, all the while waited too, but then I thought it started to become a little awkward for the others waiting.

"Hey now you guys, I'm fine see?" I pushed their chins up so that they could see my smiling face. I still struggled to put a smile on my face after everything that has happened.

"Scarlett, you look like you just got hit by a bus, and your white as a damn sheet." Sarah barely swore unless she was serious or she wanted to make a severe point.

"I'm alive and walking aren't I?" They looked back up at me, Ivy half-heartily laughed at me and wiped Sarah's tears with a tender touch and smiled at me with what seemed like a tad bit of sarcasm.

"Who gives a fuck about if you're walking or not, we are still entitled to a worry factor!" They gave Bambi a jealous and slightly snobby glare, "We are also entitled into asking who's this and why was she able to see you but we weren't?" Sarah's glare sizzled to nothing as a severe look of hurt on her face, she wouldn't speak, her eyes locked on Bambi in a vacant look of pure confusion and pain. Their expressions killed me.

I pride myself, almost noticeably, off their iron grips on my waist and arms. I turned around to find Bambi politely waiting, with an uncomfortable little pucker at her lips. I gestured towards her with my arms sweeping in a gracious circle as if I was inviting in the queen to join me and my colleagues, "This is Bambi. And no- don't be alarmed my young warriors, I have to go to her house so that she can *clinically... watch over me.*" I sighed in defeat knowing that I couldn't even try to run away because that would just waste my time and it would be harder on the both of us.

"Yeah, she will be safe and sound and as cozy as can be in my little hole I call home. Don't worry- she will be okay, I was just assigned to look over her to, uh, make sure that she is *clinically okay,* not that I think she's not okay or anything but...uh..."

She looked really uncomfortable, with her hands stuffed into her hospital sweatshirt that lingered over her hospital outfit, her whitish-yellow teeth tugging at the little rough skin patch on her lips. In a way I thought of her as a little girl in a little, puffy blue dress on a bright Sunday morning, fidgeting with her white gloves in church.

"What's wrong with us taking care of her in our dorm rooms?" Ivy looked mortified that she couldn't spend time with me after the big accident. My friends were very close to me and my mother. If anything happened the secondary person they would call is my mom or me. Friendships grow strong over the years...as you can tell from the mere stories and observation.

"They want her under a specified medical helper and or assistant, she is to not go out of my sight unless permitted for the next week otherwise after further evaluation will she be released from that medical helper and or assistant, and left with herself to be as she pleased." She recited it all as if she was reading it out of a handbook. I was a little shocked from her amazing memory, I couldn't even remember something as easy as to bring lunch money to the cafeteria so that I can eat at school. "I'm sorry, I really am- but if I don't do this I will get fired. I know how much you probably want to see your friend." Bambi gave a little shrug, her cheek dimple more pronounced as she bit her lip harder, as if trying to tell herself to keep quiet.

"Are we allowed to visit her, at least *that* much?" Ivy, for the first time I have ever seen her, let her tough girl guard down, she started to whimper and then full out started to cry in front of me. The thing with Ivy is that she is very proud of her amazing ability to

43

avoid showing any emotions. Besides anger. Ivy never cries and I have never seen her cry, because she takes out her angers by writing ferociously in her camouflage, green fuzzy journal.

She writes letters to those she is having problems with either telling them how much she hates them or telling them why they make her so upset or sad. Except the big catch is that no one will ever read those letters, and they will never be able to because it has a huge lock on it.

I am not talking about those phony little clip on locks, because I can pick one of those in minute. I am talking about a five key lock that actually covers the perimeter edges of the journal so that you can't even try to peek in the pages. She has four of the keys hidden in different places in her bedroom floorboards and one big one that hangs around her neck at all times. The top of it is cut and customized so that it is a three hole punched circle, clothing button. She loves her mass Tim Burton collection so much, but I would have to say that one of his recent movies "Coraline" has to be her top two favorites...hence the button shaped key- like in the movie. It's the absolute best accessory for her too.

"That is fine as long as I am there with her..." Bambi's voice trailed off and she sort of stood there while she saw that Ivy started to cry. Ivy barreled into my arms and she clutched me as close to her as she could.

"I thought you were *dead!*" She hiccupped the words into my shoulders, sniffling, drawing out the word *dead*. Her Coraline key slipped into my shirt. Uncomfortable, cold, and chilling, probably just like my heart. I didn't know that she could care about me this much- she hadn't even cry when her grandmother died.

"Scarlett, don't ever scare me like that ever again! You're all I have left- I cannot lose you." She just kept sobbing into my arms, I dug my face deep into her hair breathing in the contenting smell of violets and blueberries. I felt a couple cold tears run down my face and run deep into her hair, making her hair shine brighter at those little droplet spots.

I could feel my eyes widen, as I stared at the blue tiled floor. "Shh, listen- I will never go, okay? You need to know that I will never ever leave you without saying goodbye first." She pulled away and looked deep into my facial features, looking from one of my eyes to the other.

"You need to promise me that, Scarlett- your, like, my sister and I couldn't bear to lose my best friend, and family." She grabbed my shoulders, mascara smeared on my hospital clothes, and nodded, "Okay?"

"Okay." I sniffled, laughed and wiped at part of her tear stained face, "Aw, look, your make-up looks all shitty now. Sorry 'bout that."

She pulled a strand of purple hair behind her ears and giggled, "Nothing is stopping you, now is it?" She punched my shoulder lightly and sniffled loudly at me. I looked at her features with new eyes. Without all that make up on, her eyes looked like little, bright yellow stars that shown brighter than the sun, her lips were a deep, crimson red instead of the bright purple lipstick caked on every day. I haven't ever seen her without make-up on- because she even sleeps in it, so when I see her face all natural and clean like this- she looks really beautiful.

"You look hot without make up on, Ivy," I laughed and peered more at her space-like eyes, feeling myself being lost in them. Because she puts on so much eyeliner that you don't really pay attention to her eyes, and notice the fact they are really pretty.

She lifted one shoulder in a lazy shrug, "Nah, if anyone would be talking about pretty they would be talking about your fucking awesome locks!"

She pawed my hair and felt it thoroughly and then stopped abruptly to look at me suspiciously, "Wait, a couple of hours ago you had short hair...is this a joke or are you wearing a wig?" She yanked on it twice and started to get frustrated and confused, "Man that's really on there!" I ripped my hair out of her hands, my skull vibrating with pain from how hard she tried to rip the hair from my head, "And it was this freaky red color-what the hell did you do, Scarlett?" She raised one brow and her eyes widened and she squinted at my face. "You eyes changed color! Why are you wearing glasses?" All the questions gathered in my head in a jumble...I could feel a migraine coming on. Whoever the fuck Heth is, I am going to find him and I am going to kill him for making me like this...for gods sakes I don't even know *who* he was or *how* he even knows me! Ugh!

"I will explain my look later...but right now," I was peering behind them to find Romeo, Hidalgo, Nina and a bunch of kids from school, all holding bouquets of flowers with little notes of "I'm sorry" and pathetic "Get better" all over the place. Well, this is embarrassing.

My eyes met them all but I didn't know who to thank or hug first, considering whomever I *did* hug that would *not* change how embarrassing it would be if I singled someone out. I looked at all their smiling (confused but smiling) faces and sighed, a tiny smile formed at my lips and I felt my voice quiver when I spoke, "Thanks guys, really," I heard a nurse call my name behind me. Saved by the bell.

I spun around and saw the skinny blond nurse jogging towards me holding something red. When she got closer I sucked in a tiny (but very unnoticeable) breath feeling a sense of déjà vu pulling at my mind, knowing that these flowers were really important...but that they came from Heth.

"Excuse me ma'am! You forgot these!" She handed me the flowers and I knew that she should have never given them to me in front of everyone, because after she handed me the blood-red daisies a depressing sigh relieved from the crowd behind me. I sighed in defeat.

I turned around making a mental note that all of the flowers besides Romeo's and Hidalgo's were cheep drugstore flowers. Romeo Held the most beautiful bouquet of rainbow roses while Hidalgo held a beautiful handful of white rose buds that had been hand-splattered with rainbow colors of paint. I couldn't decide which one looked more gorgeous...But I felt the red daisies were the best for some reason.

This boy seemed important to me, he seemed like a mysterious version of my worst nightmare and my best dream put together. But that never changed the sincere fact that these men in front of me had something going on with me whether it was good or bad...I think that you can pull the two apart when it comes to which one I found good and which one I found bad. Duh.

Today wasn't my best day ever but I can understand how, and I know I am crazy for saying this, but for once it's like a weight having been lifted up off of my shoulders. I was not aware how all these kids cared for me.

"Thanks," I walked a little closer into the crowd and then took one of the baskets full of magazines off of a coffee table and emptied it. I went around quietly murmuring my thanks to all of my pears the best I could without breaking down. All the guys said their apologies, and then put their flowers in the basket, and most of the girls hugged me.

45

Once I got all of the flowers gathered I turned to the last ones standing and I grew tense at them both in the same room together, while I felt that familiar feeling of... territorial leadership.

I said a quick thanks to them both and carefully set their flowers on top of a couple of tiny white flowers, and hurried through it because I just wanted all of this to be over. I want to go home crawl in my bed and cry my eyes out for hours. I didn't wanna waste my time here either- I wanted to be alone. But according to the nurses, I wouldn't be granted with that wish because I was assigned a *babysitter*. I left everyone as they made their way out into the parking lot, and followed Bambi to a little orange bug. I climbed into the little snug orange bug and put the basket in the back, and drifted into a very uncomfortable car nap.

# Chapter 18

I should have known better. I read so many novels and I couldn't recognize where I was, which in fact was clearly Summerland. Or my viewing of Summerland, anyways. I was lying on a crisp white bed about the size of my bedroom floor. Fuzzy cotton and the most comfortable pillows, and silk mattress were what I was covered in and touching. I looked up and around to see the most beautiful sunlight shine so bright it hurt my eyes. I cuddled in more to my fluffy white comforter, feeling the relaxation vibes from it seep in deep to my skin. I felt love and warmth, and for the first time this whole week I felt like I was home again... I felt like I was protected by my own self being and that my heart was a growing balloon about the burst.

I sat up straight to find myself in a white dress, that had big ruffles and practically made my skin seem like it glittered. I looked over and saw a boy in white with big black wings, picking sunflowers. But every time he picked a flower, it would just turn into a blood red daisy. He looked at me and he smiled with white teeth.

He looked about my age and when he smiled at me I felt a wave of shyness swell in me. He walked over and I felt my head get hot from the sunlight shining on my black hair. I was afraid of the boy, in a way- but then he seemed safe enough.

"Hello, my Scarlett." He then held out his hand to help me out of the big bed. "The white bed symbolizes comfort and trust to you, you know. Otherwise you would have never imagined it up." I hopped out of the bed and when my bare feet hit the ground I felt warm and silky soil seep in between my toes. I smiled at the ground and then looked up with a smirk on my face.

"I know what it means." He grinned an ecstatic smile my way and let go of my hand after he squeezed it for reassurance. "I am guessing that you must be the boy who sent me the lovely red daisies?" I looked at his physic as I imagined him in dirty blue overalls for some reason, thinking about how it would be nice to touch his hair that beckoned me to him. I tested him by raising a brow.

Genuine joy crossed his face as fast as a forest fire, his slate gray eyes now silver making me catch my breath. He half-smiled at me and raised a brow, "So, I see you got them?" He circled me while he talked as if I was being evaluated.

"Yes..." I drew out the word as if I meant to keep my sentence going, but questioning him in return.

"I just *love* your new look by the way...it's so...it's so..." He stopped behind me and slid his hand down my hair, making my hot hair sizzle and chill. "You." His hands were ice cold- like sticking ice on a burn, and it felt intoxicating. He ran his fingers through it, the feel of his fingernails grazing against my skin felt ticklish, and it left me shaken, where the fingernails left my skin, were the tiny areas that that we chilled, making the rest of my body that were warmed very envious.

"You did this to me, of course you would love it." I joked but then frustration and confusion raked against my skin in pure anger. I spun around, bewildered.

"You did this to me." I looked down at the soil and started to back up, feeling the crunch of all the sunflowers poke into my feet- seeds scattering. I started to shake my head no. No- this isn't possible, I don't believe in things like this- I don't believe a boy in my dreams could physically change the way I am- the way I think. No!

He remained calm standing there, his face blank, as if waiting for me to stop. He abruptly ran towards me and took hold of my shoulders the strength of his hands

47

grounding me there. I kept turning my head away from his eyes not wanting to look him in the face, not wanting to believe any of this. Things like this weren't true. He willed me to look him in the face with his mind- I could feel the severe pushing pressure in my brain and his voice booming through the shell of my head telling me to look at him, look him in the face, but most of all to listen.

In a shaky labored voice his face got close and he started to whimper and tear up as he whispered to me. "You *have* to believe, Scarlett. Please...you just have to, okay?" When I saw the pained look on his face I could just feel my heart shatter. His eyes bored into mine, horrible feelings rushing through my head- my mind and soul felt connected to him like we were one. The feelings that he shared with me made me want to scream.

It was pure hate. And fear, and disappointment, and confusion, and horrid anger. But it never stopped- the emotions just pushed at every cent of my being.

I nodded but then I started to shake as I clutched onto his shirt and started to slowly fall to the ground. His pained expression turned into confusion, as he started so scream.

"Stop hurting her! Please just stop!" He started to cry into my dress ruffles as I lay paralyzed on the floor, not moving a muscle. I couldn't think either. All I could do was hear Heth's cries of pain as he sobbed into my dress. I didn't know what was happening but I lay there, just listening to him asking something, someone I couldn't see- to stop. He sat up and moved the hair by my ear and whispered in it.

"Scarlett, my dear, dear Scarlett. If you can hear me you need to know this. There's not just one person out there- there's two, and they are both doing bad things- and once they pick off all the people around you, you're next. Can you hear me, Scarlett? You will be next!"

I felt my body uncomfortably shift and my hand banged against something hard, like glass.

"Scarlett! What do you want? Were next!" I jumped up quickly in my seat, touching random things to make sure I was able to move. When I jumped up my head bashed against the top of Bambi's car and I rubbed my head cursing under my breath.

"What?" I asked groggily taking in my surroundings. We were at the Wendy's on First Avenue. We were getting food... oh.

"Food, Scarlett- what do you want?" She asked a little chipper. I couldn't remember my dream, but all I could remember was that by the end I couldn't move.

"Um..." I looked randomly at the menu and picked a picture. "I'll just have that," I let my eyes scan around the car and noticed that I fell asleep with the red daisies in my lap. There was an envelope on it now, with a red daisy drew on it in more red pastels. All I could think of was a name that popped into my mind.

*Heth.*

"Okay!" she smiled at me and the smell of the fast food made my stomach ache in severe hunger. As she ordered I lovingly looked at the flowers. I remember now that I'm dreaming about him, but that still doesn't answer the questions of who he is, why he is what I dream about, and why I can't remember anything about the dream once I wake up. I didn't wanna think about it too hard, so all I focused on was Bambi's cheery voice talking about how this week was going to be a blast as we waited in the car line for our food. I sat there looking impatiently ahead of me at the white fan, willing it to just move already so that I could eat something that doesn't taste like hospital sand.

I just nodded and said "Yeah," a lot so that she was sure aware that I was paying attention even though I clearly wasn't, but still- it assured her.

Finally, after what seems like ten long torturous minutes later, the car moves and we get our food. As soon as the bag is in my hand, I start taking things out and eating things out of the plastic containers like an animal. Bambi and the worker gave me an odd look but Bambi just shook her head and handed them the money, then we were off again.

"Dang were you hungry or what?" She peeked past me into the bag, "You didn't eat my food didn't you?" I looked in and saw a sandwich and little cup of fries spared. I handed them to her and she dug in.

We both ate in silence, but it wasn't awkward- we were both just really hungry for food to talk. I made my mind go numb and listened to the hum of the car mixed with the slight crunch of ice and snow from under the tires. I couldn't feel any emotion while I rustically ate. Then the silence broke after we were finished and her face was serious.

"One of the people there at the visiting hours in the hospital, said that they wanted to take a little private time of yours so that they could spend time with you. I said it was fine with me as long as it was fine with you- so they're going to be probably waiting at the house." I could hear the small squeak of her hands twisting, rubbing around the leather of the steering wheel. She seemed a little on edge and since my mind was so numb I didn't even think to ask who it was.

"Okay," I stuffed all the rappers from the food into the bag and the squeaking was getting on my nerves- it was setting *me* on edge.

"Why do you seem upset, Bambi?" I glanced over at her and felt my reddish, brown eyes pierce into her shoulder.

She sighed and shook her head, "Something about that boy rubs me the wrong way. I don't like him, not one bit. You know that feeling where your hair stands on end that you just know something isn't right? When I saw him, I got that exact feeling." I peered at her hesitantly, not knowing which boy she was talking about.

But I could tell she wanted to say something else but was clearly holding back, "And?"

"I don't think you should go with him." She was blunt to me- the first one today to be strait with me, and I respected that.

"Why not?"

"Like I said- I don't like him. I feel like he will hurt your feelings sooner or later." "How?"

"He seems like a player and I don't want you to think you're in love with him later on because he acts so great. He reminds me of Sleazy Jefferson Mason."

"Who's that?" It felt nice to talk to someone else. I realized that now when I felt I relax, but then felt guilty for doing so. My mother just died and I shouldn't be relaxing. After all this was all my fault that she died anyways- I blame myself for all of it. No one could really understand *how* much I blamed myself- they just wouldn't get it.

"He's a boy at my school who likes to sweet talk girls and make them feel all special. He would give striped carnations to his recent girl. It sickened me to the core when he would make a big deal about it- like it meant some great big thing.

"When I asked my home economics teacher what they meant just out of curiosity, she told me to look it up on the Internet, which is where I soon found out that they meant, 'I could never be with you'.

"He would be all about you- but then as soon as another girl came walking by he would sniff the air and drop you like a fly. He's such a pig and he broke a lot of girl's hearts..." Her voice trailed off and her eyes were like sharp daggers looking forward at the road, her jaw clenched. I missed the cheery Bambi that was here about a half an hour ago.

Softly and in a quiet voice I asked, "Did Jefferson do that to you, Bambi?" I could feel the frown on my face deepen when she lowered her head with tears in her eyes in defeat once we stopped at a stoplight.

A tear fell, and she sighed, driving when the light on the stoplight we stopped at turned green she rose her head and looked ahead, avoiding my face, "We're almost home...grab your flowers."

I did what she said, and set the daisies delicately onto the stack and touched one of the paint splattered white rose buds that Hidalgo gave me, some of the paint rubbed off on my fingers and as I peered down at the red paint that smeared on my thumb and index finger I thought two things to myself.

I still don't know who I am going to see later today- who I'm supposed to take a walk with.

And who is as cruel as a man to do hurt someone as lovely as Bambi? Well all I know is...he's a complete and utter jerk.

# Chapter 19

When I stepped inside her apartment, I was a little surprised but on the other hand I wasn't.
Everything was so...matched up. Like everything came straight out of a house design magazine. Hell- this *was* the magazine I was sure. I set my stuff down by the door, as I took my flats off gingerly, staring, and couldn't stop.

She giggled, "A little set off, Scarlett?" She turned around and put her hands on her hips and inhaled slowly taking it all in, then turned back to me and grabbed my bags, taking them into the other room while yelling over her shoulder, "Yep, this is home! My parents pay for designing the apartment- I pay for the bills and stuff. I thought it was quite a fair deal!" She came back and genuinely smiled at me, as if the little chat in the car never ever happened. I still couldn't help thinking what man would hurt Bambi, I mean she was so cheery, and sweet. She looks like she couldn't kill a fly.

"Yeah," Was all I was able to utter quietly under my breath, because I was so awestruck about her apartment, as lovely spring colors exploded before my eyes. Watermelon plates and pink tinted silverware. She had watermelon wineglasses for cups it looked like and everything in the room was a variation of pinks, greens, oranges, reds and yellows. This was every stay-at-home mom's dream. Even *I* found myself wanting everything in her house.

She continued on her long welcome, merrily, "You will be staying in the guestroom, there are towels and toilet paper and girly help down in the cupboard, all in the bathroom. And you know what I mean right by girly-"

"Yeah, I'm sure I got it." I felt my eyes dart back and forth across the room and started to feel uncomfortable with this conversation. No one has ever really spoke to me about that stuff since...since-

"Okay! The food pantry is stocked all up, so if you're a midnight snack person like me, you will be sure to dip in there some time...and, oh, what else am I forgetting...? Something that I forgot about...at a certain time something was going to happen...no- wait! Someone-" Then all of a sudden- the doorbell rang, and her face fell into a deep frown. I didn't feel like seeing anyone really.

Bambi briskly walked over to the door and jerked it open, with a little force I might add, and Hidalgo rushed inside without asking, chest heaving, and sweat dripping from his face onto the nice orange speckled rug.

"What in the name of god is going on? And you *aren't* the guy who asked to hang out with Scarlett, so what are you doing here?" She didn't seem mad, but not happy- more like... startled. He held up a finger to keep her quiet for a little bit- then when he had enough air to breath he spoke to her in Spanish in an urgent panic.

"*Dame un momento.*" She just stood there with the door hanging wide open, her *mouth* hanging open, and her eyes flickering back and forth from him to me as if to ask what he'd just said. I stood there as still as a statue and I exhaled realizing that I was holding my breath. It took a minute but he stood up and took both of my hands and had a cute smile planted on his face, "I came to rescue you." he giggled and I smiled slightly and cocked my head in confusion.

"Rescue me? From what exactly?" I glanced at Bambi and told her he was an okay person with my eyes. She nodded and relaxed just a bit.

"Romeo planned on spending time with you today. But to bad for him because I'm stealing you away first." I heard Bambi sigh lovingly and put a hand on her heart. I gazed at Hidalgo and realized how close we were and that his sweet breath was falling on my face. I smiled at him, unsure and then he winked at me- making me realize what I wanted to do and deciding on the spot.

"Let's go." I said slowly as if it was still being thought over. He looked at Bambi pleadingly.

"*Podemos ir, verdad?*" She just nodded and grinned, tears brimming her eyes from all the sweetness.

He pulled me out the door but Bambi pulled me back and turned me to face her, shoved two mints in my mouth, fixed my hair, lifted my pits, checked 'em and then whispered, "Your good!" to me before Hidalgo yanked me from her grip and we ran off, jumping fences and crossing many backyards.

We giggled at all the excitement and I felt like Juliet being pulled away by her Romeo- but from a *different* Romeo in this case. Hypothetically. Finally, we came to the tent in the park and I suddenly knew what he had in store for me.

# Chapter 20

"No. I'm *not* going to do that. *No.*" I stood there with my hands on my hips, giving him a stern look, but having a hard time *not* thinking about how beautifully tan he looks. We went through some casual dance moves that I sort of already knew from the movies I rented. Back and forth little motions that were easy- not too mortifying. But then he wanted to try another dance move with me that was past my comfort zone.

"*Mi dios*...Scarlett you need to feel comfortable with me in order for me to teach you how to dance, or you won't be able to learn and feel it." He sighed and closed the three feet between us. His big brown eyes locked on my chest and then I felt insecure and embarrassed and appalled. I was just about to say something when he stuck his hand on my heart. Thank Jesus that was his true intention.

"It's like the thumping of your heart. Feel your heart thumping. Transfer it into the beat when your dancing. Dance with your heart, and with your soul, ignore the thoughts in your mind." He patted my chest, the rhythmic *thud-ump thud-ump-ump thud-ump thud-ump-ump.* Then I could hear the faint thumping along with the sound of him patting my heart. He put both of his hands on my hips and I hitched a breath. He just tightened his grip a little and then looked at me and nodded with confidence. Gradually he shook them back and forth faster, tighter. To the beat I shook my hips in his grip like I was trying to melt his hands into my hips. Back and forth, back and forth.

His smile got bigger and bigger, "Yes, good, Scarlett- your doing it, your dancing!" I couldn't help but give him a small smile at his appraising. After a couple minutes a hesitant guarded look overtook his face.

"Are you ready to go a little farther? Because, Scarlett, were moving at an extremely low pace and if your going to learn this we need to move on from just shaking back and forth." My smile disappeared as fast as it appeared and I felt a pout come on my face and then my expression became hard and guarded once again.

"What are you talking about when you mean 'go a little bit farther'?" I stopped shaking and just stood there awkwardly with his hand on my hips. He didn't move though so it must have seemed natural to him.

He just gave a hesitant look and then took a step closer so that our noses almost touched. His breath that fell on my face- it was electric. I, all of a sudden, wanted to kiss him so bad. Man...if I'm thinking like this now- I can't imagine how I will be able to dance with him like *that* without feeling *something* in between us two. He relaxed his grip on my hips a little and then nodded once, "Are you ready, *chica?*" He still has that hesitant look on his face but like he said I had to trust him.

"Show me what to do." I noted to myself that I said *show* instead of *tell.* Probably because I knew whatever it was- I wasn't going to be too comfortable with.

He started up with the shaking again and I relaxed my muscles when I heard him mutter, "Scarlett, your too tense- just let go." I felt myself close my eyes and listen to my heart beating with the music in my ears. When I opened my eyes, Hidalgo had a small determined grin on his face, "Get into your comfort zone, are you ready?" I nodded a little scared and focused on his beautiful brown eyes. Then with such quickness his hands scrunched up the back of my shirt and then grabbed onto a part of my waist with one hand grabbed my thigh with the other and ran his hand up it my skirt, scrunching it up as well. I saw him and then I saw my dad and I ripped out of his soft grip, scared like hell.

"Stop! Stop! Just stop!" I grabbed my head and squeezed my eyes shut and hummed to myself mentally. He rushed over to me and gave me a hug, as if extremely worried and apologized to me.

"Scarlett, I'm so sorry! What did I do?" He pulled away and looked into my teared up eyes. "Tell me what is wrong." I looked into his eyes that were wide with worry, and possibly fear.

"I love how you are teaching me how to dance...but I have gone through personal things in my life that scarred me for awhile... and when you did that- it just brought back the worst memories," I looked down at my outstretched black hair forgetting it was there.

"Sorry I freaked out on you, it's just...." I shuddered and closed my eyes and hummed my song in order for the thoughts to go away.

He frowned like his face couldn't have done anything else. He was still beautiful, his eyes just held more fear this time than worry. Although I had a feeling he feared rather *for* me than of me.

"I am so sorry, I didn't know. I won't push you any farther in this, because dancing is very physical and I do not want you to think about such terrible things that happened." He looked very glum and sad when he backed away a step.

I felt like crying all over again. I didn't want what my dad did get in the way of things in my life. I wasn't going to let that happen. He's already ruined a big part of my life- I'm not going to let him ruin another.

I took that step back and stood there in front of him looking at both of his eyes. I spoke my mind out to him because I felt that I could really trust him.

"I am not going to stop something very important to me in life because of what someone did to affect me. I'm not going to let it take over my whole life- and this is one of these moments. What you did- it just needs to go a bit slower. I like this- us, dancing. For the first time I feel free on different levels that I haven't experienced and I would like to keep it that way. So, please, just dance with me. But this time, a little slower?" He stared at me a moment and took another half-step closer and smiled sadly.

"*Creo que te gusta mucho.*" He looked at my lips for a split second and then back to my eyes. He lifted his hand in the air, and his smile twitched a little bit, "Dance with me, Scarlett." I glanced at his hand and then slipped my palm in his, intertwining my fingers with his. I smiled again. I smiled so much today day.

He took me in the rain and this time...we went a little slower.

# Chapter 21

We both lay on the picnic blanket that we found with some other contents under the tent. Me and Hidalgo, breathing real hard because of how much dancing we did. He smiled tiredly, as I remember that he probably never slept through the night. His arms spew above his head, his right arm brushing against mine. His eyelids flutter a little, growing heavy, and his breathing gets deep and slow. He was very close to sleep, and I took it as my chance to tell him how much I appreciated him.

I rolled over on my side, my clumpy, wet black hair sticking to my skin a little, still damp from all the water it soaked up. I put my head in my hand and watch as his chest rises and falls. I scoot over a little and stick my mouth up to his ear, a soft smile on my lips. "Hidalgo." His weak smile twitched a little, in response to tell me he was only half listening.

"Yes, Scarlett?" His voice was soft and a little husky from the slumber creeping in, his hushed tone telling me that he was in no state to have a longing conversation.

I smiled in response to his sleepy tone, "I want to thank you, *so* much for doing this with me. You were the light that trickled a little in my dark day today." I felt my smile tug down a little at how sad I still was. I couldn't really understand how I went on without my mother, knowing that she wouldn't be at home, and waiting for me anymore. I still didn't understand what made me sane.

"Scarlett, you will forever be my sun in my sky. Every moment I see your smiling face." He smiled a little, not realizing how pain-strikingly honest he was being with me. He slipped his arm down to his side and grabbed my free hand and softly squeezed it, telling me that he really was there. I felt my insides melt just a little with the pure trust I put in this boy sitting next to me.

*Don't trust anyone...*

My mother's words that sailed into my mind made my growing smile falter a little bit. I couldn't trust anyone. *Don't trust anyone.*

It still didn't change how content I was so I leaned in a little bit into his shoulder and relaxed, letting myself lay there in his arm. His grip around my waist tightened a little bit, telling me he was comfortable and content himself.

I forcefully closed my eyes, not tired at all because of my car ride and let my mind go numb again, not wanting to think about anything that may have been going on in my life. Nothing that may change my timeline. I just concentrated on how comfortable Hidalgo's hot arm felt on my cheek, how he was just so warm and cuddly that he should be the teddy bear I hug when I go to sleep at night. I heard the trees tussle and shivered, causing hidalgo to instantly hug me tight and rap the blanket around us. I smiled and felt a happy hum erupt from deep inside my chest. Hidalgo chuckled a little and buried his face deep in my hair, mumbling things I couldn't catch.

He moved his cheek a little so his words came more pronounced to my ears as he mumbled his last words.

"Scarlett...I like you so much." He sighed sleepily again and I sunk deeper into the blanket and his arms.

"I like you too, Hidalgo." I smiled and tapped my index finger on a little spot of his bare skin that poked out of his muscle shirt. He dipped his head down a little so that I could see his white teeth, in that biggest tired smile I have ever seen come from his face. I settled in his arms and decided to dose off.

I woke up from my dosing-off from a jolt I felt come from Hidalgo.

"What the fuck!" Romeo sat there, leaning down towards Hidalgo in a crouch, his face in his personal space, all in Hidalgo's face. Hidalgo jumped and an instant scowl screwed up on his face as he spat something in Spanish at Romeo. Romeo shook his head the whole time, eyes narrowed, while his hair jiggled around. Once Hidalgo angrily shouted his last words right in his face, Romeo smirked at him annoyingly, unfazed.

"I don't give a flying *fuck* that I woke you up. What the hell is your business taking the time that I purposely planned with her- and doing whatever the hell you want? That's bullshit!" Romeo stood up and I broodingly stared up, what seemed like as high as the clouds, at his face. Hidalgo swiftly stood up as well, getting up in his personal space like Romeo did with him, and glanced up at him, seeming he was a couple inches shorter than Romeo. Hidalgo glared at him with hard intent on pissing him off.

"Scarlett and I were *dancing*. We planned it earlier yesterday morning, you can even ask her *yourself.*" A couple flecks of spit landed on Romeo's face and he wiped them off and smeared them on Hidalgo's shirt. Romeo leaned over to his side to take a look at me, and his face lit with a questioning look.

I immediately stood up and tucked a big chunk of my frizzy hair out of my face and behind my ear, glaring at Romeo as well. "Calm the fuck down. Hidalgo isn't lying- I did talk to him about it first. Now calm the heck down you two- especially *you.*" I outstretched my arm and pointed directly at Romeo before stepping forward and parting the two with my arm. "Cool it."

"It's not my fault you love hanging out with in consistent pretty boys." Romeo took a step forward and glowered down on Hidalgo, who in fact was shorter- but had a stronger build. Hidalgo stayed composed- not showing any factor of losing his cool. He didn't move and just stood there while Romeo, who's protective and possessive stance was towering over Hidalgo, stood there and gave him a nasty, mean stare.

"It's not her fault that she doesn't love hanging out with provocative smart asses." Hidalgo's voice was steady and I noticed his muscles tense, his jaw tighten, and his fists squeeze. I felt my throat flex and my mouth go dry knowing that this doesn't seem to be going into a correct direction.

"Hidalgo, how about you go run home and take care of your family because your drunk ass mother can't." Romeo smirked at him easily, aware that he already went too far but proud of himself because he did.

I couldn't blink before I saw a flash and Hidalgo was on top of Romeo on the floor, straddling him and holding his wrists down above his head.

"Don't you ever fucking talk about my family again or so help me god I will beat you down until your six feet under!" His face was in Romeo's screaming at the top of his lungs. "*Usted Culo desconsiderado! Nunca se habla de mí o de mi vida personal de nuevo!*" I tore Hidalgo's body off of Romeo's and he jerked from my grasp and ran off into the distance. I back up a couple steps, watching Hidalgo's running body fade into the foggy haze. I spun around to glance at Romeo standing up, my face mortified. My emotions were a cross of pure anger and hurt. I was so mad at him for making Hidalgo go away and I was hurt that Hidalgo ran away, but I knew none of this was his fault. It was all Romeo's. It always seemed to be his fault all the time.

"*Je vous hais! Vous êtes une telle secousse, j'espère vous tombez dans un trou et affamer!*" I shouted at the top of my lungs at him.

His eyes widened and his mouth went agape- "Did you just...yell in *French* at me?" I felt the breath leave my lungs and my eyes flutter. I gripped my heart and took a couple more steps back scared and confused.

"I-I don't know French...I-I have no idea how I just *did* that...*w-what*?" I started to hyperventilate. I- what? How was that even possible? I never spoke or heard a word in French my whole life! What- how-?!

"Scarlett- you just yelled at me *in French*. What- how? W-what?!" His eyes were still bugging, his words stuttering. His arms sticky with sweat- probably from running his way here or something like that.

"I...I need to go." I ran off into the same direction that I took to get to the tent, and quickly made my way across some back yards, but then found myself taking a different route. I turned right instead of left and ran as fast as I could, letting my mind lead me where I need to be, closing my eyes and mindlessly running- not knowing where I am going.

I found myself in a grave yard, when I opened my eyes. I was standing in front of a grave that was ginormous. It wasn't just any normal tombstone- it was a statue. A statue of a man with wings curling around his body, and a pain-stricken expression on his face, almost as if he is trying to protect himself. I bent down to read the text on the engraved part of the statue, but my bulky glasses slid down my nose and fell off my face and onto the mushy grass.

I patted the ground, unaware of where they may have fallen, and then felt my fingers brush on plastic rimming. I grabbed the glasses and hesitated slightly when I heard a male chuckle. The breath on the back of my neck made my hair drift slightly. The breath was warm in this cold day, I felt Goosebumps on my arms- the effect it left.

"Silly...silly...Scarlett." He breathed the words into the crane of my neckline. It wasn't Hidalgo- nor was it Romeo. This voice was...mysterious. *Dark.*

No scratch that. *Mischievous.*

He grabbed my glasses, reached out from behind me, and then his cold arms brushed against mine as he put them on my eyes.

I could see clearly and then looked down at the engraved letters.

"Here lies Heth Blakeley" I felt my world come crashing down on me, hard. I couldn't breathe.

I heard him chuckling behind me again, darkly, and then he moved the black hair from behind my ear, and whispered to me, his wispy words tickling the inside of my ear.

"I'm dead," He said happily- lightly, almost humorously, and then he started laughing darkly behind me again.

57

# Chapter 22

"Scarlett you need to wake up- we fell asleep. I need to get you home!" Hidalgo shook me lightly, urgently whispering to me. I heaved in a breath and sat up strait. I took a few moments to collect my thoughts.

There was *no way* that I was dreaming.

"I need to get you home, *chica,* now! I was supposed to have you home about an hour ago!" His eyes were filled with fear and his movements were twitchy and frantic. I finally comprehended what he was saying and I felt fear swell in my chest and in my heart.

"Oh...Oh my god! We need to go!" I nodded and stood up as fast as I could.

"Yes! We do- let's *go!*" He grabbed my hand and we ran back to Bambi's house, jumped all the same fences, and flew our way across the same back yards, through several parks, until we finally saw her dot of a house in the distance.

"There! I see her house!" I yelled, my sides aching- my pace slowing down. He nodded and painfully dragged me along anyways. We padded across her lawn and ran though the door, to find Bambi standing there with her hands on her hips and her foot tapping rapidly.

"Where the devil's name have you two *been*?!" She shouted at us.

"I- we- us-" I stuttered trying to find the right words but not seeming to speak complete sentences. Hidalgo cut in, trying to help me out, his face as panicked as I felt. "I-"

"*We* both fell asleep, and we lost track of time- Bambi, I am *so sorry* that I didn't bring her home in time." He slowed his breathing and lowered his head in shame.

Bambi's rigid posture slouched a little bit, she sighed and I saw guilt cross her face. She looked at the carpet pattern, thinking about whether she should still be mad, or feel guilty for yelling at us. "I...Scarlett, I can get fired if I don't watch you right- and if I get fired, I can't pay my bills." She shoved her hands in her pockets and gave me an irritated look, "My life right now? It's all on you." I felt my heart crush at her words. I didn't really want to be the thing that made her life count. I didn't want to be that person to have to save her job. I didn't want to be that person who made her living, that she payed her bills with possible. I didn't want more stress on me, let alone on others that I caused to be possible. I didn't want this- I didn't want my life right now.

"I am so sorry. I- we...we didn't realize how stupid it was of us to fall asleep- for now on, I will behave how you need me to the next week. And if I need to go somewhere- I will take you with me," I sighed roughly, "As the hospital orders you to." I felt my irritation grow at this, but didn't show it as loud on my outer shell.

"Thank you, that all I ask."

"Never again will I disobey your rules- my mother taught me better than that." Hidalgo's head was still lowered and I felt my irritation dim with the sadness of Hidalgo's face.

"It's alright...uh-"

"Hidalgo." He smile a little, and Bambi put on a weak smile in response, and nodded awkwardly with her hands still in her pockets.

"Yeah, it's..." She exhaled slowly, "It's...okay." She cringed at him and me, "Just-don't...don't let it happen again, okay?" We both nodded in response. "Well, okay- time for you to go Hidalgo, I have to talk to Scarlett privately- it was very nice to meet you though," She gave him a genuine grin and he smiled lightly in response.

"Likewise, Bambi." He sighed and turned away to leave- took one look at me and came very close. I could feel my heart pounding in my chest, as he stepped so close and leaned in. I hitched a breath in time to have his face tilt a little to the side and continued leaning in until his mouth was at my ear to whisper. I felt like an idiot when he started whispering in my ear- me thinking he was going to kiss me was the stupidest thought in the world. "I will come back to teach you more dancing- if I have to sneak you out, I will. Bye-bye, *chica.*"

I blushed so hard it was ridiculous, I tried turning away really quick after nodding so he wouldn't see me- but of course since its Hidalgo he sees every move I make.

He leaned in again and whispered in my ear again, smiling so big and chuckling.

"Wanna know a secret?" I pulled away for a moment and nodded real quick and listened to him again. He lowered his voice to barely a whisper, "You're really cute when you try to hide your blushes." I pulled away and put a hand on my cheek, which was hot and smiled a little, stumbling over my words.

"I- uh...Sorry." I cursed myself on the inside for being such an idiot.

"Why are you apologizing?"

"I...uh...I don't know I guess. Ha." I backed away a couple steps when I saw Bambi staring at us.

He chuckled and waved goodbye as he shut the door behind him.

Once he was out of earshot and about a block away, Bambi *screamed* at the top of her lungs, to the point where her neighbors started yelling. I jumped and clutched my heart- and yelled at her.

"Bambi! *What the hell?*" She just continued this horribly cheesy grin on her face and covered her mouth, trying to calm down. She giggled and squealed again, jumping up and down. She started to do a little conga line towards me, and took my hands and dragged me around the room, dancing- she let go and started dancing on her own- shaking her hips.

She yelped again, "*World*! Scarlett's found love with a boy named *Hi-*!" Just in time, I ran over and put my hand over her mouth- only resulting in her licking it and me letting go.

"Ew! Gross! Nasty! Bambi- I haven't found love! I dance with the boy for Christ sake!" I wiped my hand off on my shirt bunches of times and then went to wash my hands in the sink, she just followed me, not letting the idea go.

59

"You *love* him! I can see it in those little- er, I can't decipher what color your eyes are." I scrubbed harder, my veins popping out.

"Forget it."

"Forget what- the eyes or the *boy*?" She smiled and flinched a little at how red my hands were from scrubbing. "Hey, you like a germaphobe or something?"

"Both and No."

"Then why are you scrubbing your hands like you have·crap plastered on them, Scarlett?" Stress mechanism. I could tell.

I rinsed my burning hands, rubbed red, and shook them off yelling at her. "Nothing! Okay? I have nothing to say about Hidalgo and his eyes...wait w-" Bambi's eyes lit up like she just got a good cookie. She smiled and pointed at me, jabbing her finger into my shoulder, lightly pushing me playfully.

"There! Ha! You see- I got off the subject there and you just swept back in it! You can't stop thinking about him, you dirty liar!" She smiled bigger, strait teeth happily showing themselves, tipping her arms and clapping quickly like she won a prize at the fair.

"Your not being fair, Bambi! Nothing was going on there okay?" She gave an amused sarcastic look.

"Yeah, like that huge *blush* on your face helps *anything*!" She pushed me on the shoulder again, "You were shamelessly flirting with him *right in front of me* and you know it!" I couldn't help but smile, because I realized that this is the most positive interaction with a boy since I first met Shane. I felt my smile vanish.

"I shouldn't be thinking about boys." I said monotonously. I went over to her couch and hugged my legs to my chest. "My mom just died yesterday." I buried my face into my legs and started sobbing. I heard sock muted footsteps padding over to me and felt myself lean to the side a little bit from Bambi dragging the cushions down. I leaned on her and she tugged on my arm telling me to come into her arms. I hugged her while she shushed me, and wailed.

On the radio that was playing on her computer in the background, *Dreams* by *The Cranberries* was playing in the background, which seemed to sound like the perfect music, her high pitched voice, the soft guitar, the tambourine softly tapping in the background. It seemed to be her theme song for this moment- forgetting the lyrics.

"Wait here, she slowly let me go, not before giving me a reassuring small rub on the back. She disappeared into the kitchen, and rummaged around in the cabinets. The song in the background changed to *Breathe* by *Anna Nalick*. All together this matched my feeling right now. I listened to her beautiful voice telling me to 'just breathe'. Bambi came out of the kitchen with a pack of Oreo Cookies and Peanut Butter. One movie popped in my head:

*The Parent Trap.*

She gave me a little smile and sat down next to me. She looked a little sheepish as she sat down next to me and peered down at the oddball combination. She started to speak, but didn't look up at me.

"You know, there's only one movie out there that is my absolute favorite. Ever since I was younger. That, my friend, is *The Parent Trap*." She gave me another sheepish and embarrassed smile. Her eyes bored into mine as she spoke with a passion about the film.

"I was...*obsessed* with that movie actually. And-" She exhaled loudly and got up, going over to the entertainment center. She grabbed a very cracked, bent, stained movie case, but when she opened it up- the disk was pristine in quality on the front. She shuffled back over and hopped onto the couch, and pulled the disk out of its case. "I own three copies." She smiled down at the movie in soft adoration. "This is just one of the copies. The other two are back-ups if anything goes wrong with this one, and I would have to say- this one looks like its reaching its expiration date." She pulled the pristine disk out of the case, and turned it over revealing some hardcore amount of scratches, fingerprints, and cracks. I peered down at the horror of a movie disk, eyes wide with tears rimming them- water droplets sticking to my glasses. She glanced back up at me, back at the movie, and back at me again. "This is the same movie that I would play when my mom decided to drink when she had a bad day." She said softly, "Since I was an only child, I yearned for that twin that I would meet at some girls camp. I begged god for someone to come and save me, and eventually someone did. My dad." She sighed. "I lived with my dad for ten years before I moved in here, and went to the community college taking courses, and getting my bachelors degree in Sociology. I found out he now has a girlfriend and never told me. I and he haven't really spoken much since." She sighed and looked down at the Peanut Butter and cookies again. She smiled, "But one thing I *have* learned, was that when having a hard time- you give into your little weaknesses and mine, is Oreos and Peanut Butter- just like in *The Parent Trap*. So long story short, I got this for me- and this-" She pulled out a little plastic container of Black Forest Gummy Worms, "This, is what is for you." I grabbed them from her hands and blinked at her for a second.

"H-....How did you know these were my favorite?" she smiled, at me.

"Sarah and Ivy picked them up for you and told me personally to give them to you when you had the time. They know you were feeling down- so they got these for you. When you feel like it- you should give them a call, their quite worried about you." She said softly. I dropped the Gummy Worms on the coffee table and hugged her, abruptly, really tight.

"Thank you." I whispered to her.

*A Case Of You* by *Joni Mitchell* was playing in the background.

I think I could drink a case of Bambi right about now.

*"'Love is touching souls'*
*Surely you touched mine"*

Lyrics belted out the speakers and I suddenly knew that Bambi will stay in my life, even after this whole babysitting week is over.

# Chapter 23

"You know, I used to think that Dennis Quaid was so hot." I lifted my head off of Bambi's lap, giving her a funny look.

"Your not talking about the *dad* are you?" My hair lay in a pile in her lap, flopping in front of my glasses.

"Heck yes, I am talking about the dad!" I flopped back into her lap, wiping the left over mascara off my glasses lenses, from earlier before.

"You're *kidding* right?"

"Nope, I was 12- I haven't discovered boys just yet!" I glanced back at the screen where "Hallie" (really Annie's) Dad, Nick Parker, was running to hug Hallie (really Annie) at the airport.

I cocked my head to the side, "I guess, I mean if I haven't seen any one more hot than him... but him? Really, Bambi? Really?" I looked back at her, while she popped in another peanut butter covered Oreo. I winced at her because of how nasty that was.

"Hey, it's just the way life works out for little girls like me, at the time- didn't you have a crush on a celebrity in your favorite movie?" She glanced down at me and I gnawed on another Black Forest Worm.

"Yeah, I did now come to think of it." I smiled at the thought, "I forgot his name but he had long blackish brown hair, and the most beautiful green eyes I have ever seen. I loved his smile, it made me blush- even on a television screen." I cringed and looked back up at her with a yellow and orange Gummy Worm in my cheek, "But I know he wasn't anything *close* to *Dennis Quaid*." I said his name, thinking about how anyone could call him hot.

"Oh really- what movie was *your* crush from." I blushed.

"I would rather not say."

"Tell me!" I sighed.

"I am not going to say, because I don't exactly remember."

Bambi gave me an odd look, biting off another piece of cookie. "Okay, so let me get this straight." he chewed for a minute, holding up a finger telling me to wait. She swallowed and then picked at her teeth with her tongue "You like a man, who you can't remember, in a movie, that you can't remember- and you expect him to be as real to me as Dennis Quaid? He sounds so completely made up! You can't tell me that you don't remember anything from your childhood?" She smiled a little and giggled, I stared off into space.

"Actually, I barely remember anything about my childhood. Like I don't remember what elementary school I went to." Bambi stopped giggling and gave me another weird look.

"Um, weird."

"Yeah, I don't know why, really." Lie.

"Well did anything traumatic happen to you when you were younger?" She popped the rest of the cookie in her mouth.

"Nope, not that I can remember, no." Lie.

"Your lying, Scarlett." I blinked a couple times at her.

"Um, what?"

"You roll your eyes every time you lie. It's really quick and subtle, I didn't even notice it at first." I glanced up at her, and she nodded.

"I am *not* lying." She cocked her head to the side and gave me an annoying look of sarcasm.

"Your eye is twitching faster than when my daddy ran from that jackrabbit that was in my backyard when I was 7 and a half. You *are* lying."

I felt my face fall- "Lets just not talk about it okay? I don't really like to think about it."

"Is it serious?" Her voice fell silent.

"Yes, very- but I don't want to talk about it, okay? Let's do something- let's go out. Let's- Oh I know, let's call Ivy and Sarah!" I smiled and her face cringed.

"Uh, Scarlett- I got the strong impression that they didn't like me..."

"And here's your chance to bond with them- common Bambi, for me?"

She shook her head, "Eh, I don't know, Scarlett."

"Please," I sat up and entwined my fingers with her, "Bambi- I will love you *forever*, I just need a girls night- it will be like one big sleepover." She looked down at her hands.

"Why do I have a bad feeling in my stomach while thinking about this?"

"Was that a yes?"

"It's not a yes."

"Well is it a no?"

"No-" She stood up, "I just- I don't know about this, I mean they looked at me like they wanted to rip my face off earlier in the hospital!" I hugged my knees, giving her puppy dog eyes.

"Common, Bambi- I have no reason to live right now. I literally don't have *any reason to live*." Bambi's line of a mouth turned into a full blown frown.

"Now, you see, that's not fair, Scarlett, that's not fair to me- that's not fair to you, that's manipulation." I fell to the floor in front of her, grabbing her ankles, yelling at her.

"Bambi- I thought you loved me!" She sighed, and tried walking- surprisingly dragging me along easily.

"Scarlett- *Get up!*" I tightened my grip.

"Not until you say *yes* to having the girls over!"

"Are you two years old or...?"

"22!"

"*Let go!*"

"*No!*"

"Yes! *Now, Scarlett!*"

"No! Not until you say yes!"

She let out a labored breath, "*Fine, already!*"

I let go, smiled- hugged her tight, kissed her on the cheek, "Thank you!"

She rolled her eyes in response to my kind thanks, "The phones over there." She grunted and flopped herself on her couch, mumbling some things into the cushion. I just waved her off and grabbed a really cool looking strawberry phone. I opened it and dialed the seed-shaped numbers to Sarah's phone.

*Bring! Bring! Br-*

"Hello?" Sarah's tiny soft voice almost whispered into the phone.

"Hey, Sare. It's Scarlett."

"I figured you were going to call me sooner or later, but actually you called at a bad time." I heard a male voice in the background mumble.

"Uh, who's that you're with?" She coughed, and I felt my eyebrows shoot up.

"Uh, what?"

"Who are you with, Sarah?"

"Oh, no one- my little brother just has some friends over and I am at my parent's house, so..." She sighed.

"Oh, well- I called to ask you to come visit me, along with Ivy tonight- like old times, have, oh jeez this is going to sound corny, but I was wondering if you could sleep over?" I heard her hesitate into the receiver. She stayed silent for a minute.

"That would be great, Scarlett. Did you call Ivy already?" I shook my head but, knowing she couldn't see me, I verbally answered her.

"Nope, I was just going to video chat her now, Bambi has a computer- I'm not sure she would mind."

"Oh, well, Okay- I will get stuff together, I just have to, uh..." More male mumbling.

"Seriously, Sarah, who *is* that?"

"I- uh, I have to go. See you." I opened my mouth to speak but was met with a dial tone blaring in my ear.

"Weird." I sauntered over to her computer, and adjusted the camera and turned on a video chat website. Bambi, stayed where she was, face down, still mumbling into the pillow. I didn't have any trouble telling Ivy to turn on her video chat, because like always she already had it pulled up. It was her phone, since she didn't have a mobile phone and she didn't have a home phone at the dorm. I clicked on her name and heard the generic ringing. In no time, her figure was leaning forward to camera, cleavage showing, army underpants flaunted, with only a big Cardinal Capri Collage sweatshirt hanging off her shoulders.

"Go for Ivy, *chica*." She smiled at the camera, and sat in her spiny chair. "Whats up, you doing okay?" I smiled at the camera and adjusted my glasses.

"Yeah I'm doing good, just got off the phone with Sare, Actually." I glanced down at my hands and Ivy gave me a weird look and ruffled her ridiculously big, purple hair. I couldn't tell if it was just her bead head or if she teased it really big, I assumed bed head.

"Why the odd face?"

"I heard some guy in the background... she wouldn't tell me who it was either. She just gave me some bogus excuse that it was her little brother's friend and that she was at her parent's house."

"Do you think she has a boyfriend?" Ivy said, and I stopped furrowing my brow and gave the camera a blank face.

"Oh my god, that's probably what she's hiding. Sarah- having a boyfriend?" I hitched a breath at the thought. My dream, Sarah, fingernail marks.

"Yeah, maybe dude." She shrugged.

"This is giving me a bad feeling at the pit of my stomach." Ivy rolled her eyes and scratched her arm, little red freckles flushing.

"Sarah can take care of herself, Scarlett- we aren't her mother." She got up from her chair and ripped off her shirt, her grey camouflage bra riding up. She threw on a big t-shirt and some boy shorts, then yanked her pretty hair into a ponytail, but not after brushing through it first.

She threw a toothbrush in her mouth and brushed her teeth at the sink while I kept complaining and worrying. "I don't know Ivy, I just have one of those feelings again." Ivy spit out her toothpaste and rushed over to the camera with white foam all over her mouth still.

"Oh no, little bitch- you aren't screwing with one of your 'feelings' anymore. Remember last time?" She raised her eye brows and got closer to the camera. "Mark Fisher still doesn't have any chest hair because of you."

"Ouch Ivy, seriously hit a nerve there." I took my glasses off and cleaned them, Ivy's face becoming a purple mass. "It wasn't my fault that he had some bad chest acne that looked like potential mushroom fungi, I was just trying to help the guy out." Ivy got even closer to the camera.

"Yeah, and now every time you get close to him, his walking speeds up to a sprint. Dude- listen to me, no- promise me. No more interfering."

I shrugged. "Fine."

"Anything else you wanna ask or talk to me about?" She swiveled back and forth picking at her nails.

"Oh yeah! The whole reason for me calling you. I want you to sleep over tonight- Sarah's coming too."

Sarah stopped picking her nails and waggled her eye brows. "Corny much?" I sighed and laughed, my face falling in my palm.

"Yeah, I know- but still. It will be fun, promises." She chewed on her lip and swiveled some more.

"Okay, yeah. Skipping school? So in the mood!" I stopped jiggling my leg.

"No- Ivy, wait if you've got-"

"Too late! Bye, Scar-scar!" I hesitated long enough for her to click off my screen. I sighed and rubbed my face.

"What biff ill hay heap?" I spun around to see Bambi, still faced down on the pillow.

"What the hell did you just say?" I had a little burst of giggles, and she lifted her head- bed face printed on her cheeks and forehead. She glared at me and laid her head back down on the side.

"What if they hate me?" She puffed out her lips and blew up, sending her bangs awry.

"Quit stressing, okay? Everything will just be fine- you just need to take a deep breath, chill, eat something that satisfies you if the cookies and peanut butter didn't fill you up. They will like you- because I like you, and if they don't, they will just have to get over it." She smiled at me brightly, and pushed a hair out of her eyesight.

"You're the coolest take-home I have ever had, Girl." I shrugged all cute like to play it off, and flipped my hair and snapped my fingers at her.

"*You know it, girlfriend!*" She giggled and I laughed too brushing through my hair with my fingers.

"So like, how much money do you have?" Bambi twirled a hair and then set it on her lip as a mustache.

I kept pawing through my hair and put a mustache on me too, "Some- why? You aren't going to make me start paying rent are you?" She giggled and got an evil twist in her brow, shimmying her shoulders to see if her hair sparkled like mine did in the sunlight.

"You haven't had a real sleepover until you have had one with me." I squeaked my chair over and over by swiveling back and forth. "What do you usually do at your sleepovers with them?" I smiled and laughed thinking back to the last time.

"Sarah is obsessed with Jake Gyllenhaal so we spent the whole night eating cheese balls and commenting on how we could use his abs as sushi plates. It was actually funny and fun for how lame it sounds. We washed ourselves in pity." Bambi rolled her eyes and sighed roughly, twirling her hair through her fingers and sitting up, cross-legged, making the couch's leather fart.

"Is that the most fun you have ever had at a sleepover you guys planned? Eating cheese balls and watching movies?" I stopped squeaking and dropped my hair from the lips that I was puckering out.

"Is there anything more fun when you're broke?" Bambi rolled her eyes and started to violently twirl her hair with the other fingers.

"How much money do you have?"

"Seventy."

"That's little?"

"In college? Yes."

"We're spending it. I have money too." I raised my eyebrows.

"Were just spending it? You just say so? It my money dude!"

She cocked her head, "Do you want this to turn out well or do you want it to be awkward as hell?! Pick you choice!"

I sighed and took the wad out of my coat pocket. "Fine."

She perked up and grabbed the wad. "Thanks! And now with seventy plus two hundred and thirty....that makes three hundred bucks of spending money!" I got up and snatched the money counting.

"How the fuck did you get two-thirty?!" Bambi shrugged.

"My bills aren't titanic- I always have spending money." She smiled brightly and chewed on her lip, and snatched it back.

"So what are we going to do for this amazing plan for it to go well?" I plopped back on the couch. She parked next to me.

"You'll see!" She was offering me a plain Oreo when there was a knock on the door.

# Chapter 24

"I got it." I shoved the cookie Bambi gave me, in my mouth and opened the door-almost choking on the hard chunks that I ate when I came face to face with Romeo at the door.

"Hey." He had his hands shoved in his dark jean pockets in the back and I felt like fainting and puking at the same time. His face healed a little more and his hair was perfectly in place. His huge black eyes were sparkling with joy and his smirk evolved into a smile when he awkwardly scratched the back of his head. I couldn't come up with something rude to say, and I didn't want to say anything nice to him, so all I could do was stand there and give him a blank look.

"Hi."

"I, uh, spoke to...Barbie?"

"It's Bambi."

"Yeah, Bambi, about hanging out with you?"

So this was the boy- this was the one she didn't like and got bad feelings about. Brownie points for Bambi for noticing it too!

"Oh you did." I glanced back at Bambi who was glaring at her hands while she picked her nails in silence. "Bambi?" She raised her head and painted on a fake smile.

"Yeah?"

"Didn't you tell me something about someone who wanted to see me?" She nodded.

"Yeah, but I was a little confused when that other boy came by earlier."

Pow! Romeo's face fell and I didn't know why- but I wanted to yell at Bambi for being mean to him.

"Uh, what." Romeo dropped his gaze to the floor, he stopped biting his lip. His smile turned back into a smirk and he chuckled sarcastically.

"I'm going to go..." He spun around to leave and sighed and I grabbed his shoulder, after chasing him out the door. He stopped and rose his eyebrows, "No its fine- you are busy."

"No, I'm not." I pulled on his shoulder so he would face me, and found that we were at the end of the sidewalk coming up to Bambi's house.

"But, she just said-"

"I'm not busy." What was I doing? Why was I being nice to him?! I *do not* like him! No- I hate him! Stop! What? No- I need to stop this!

I took my hand off his shoulder and rubbed my arm. "What did you want to do?"

He increased his smirk and he took a step back, "I want to teach you something." I smiled awkwardly at him. "No, it's not gross."

"Oh, okay." He gave me an awkward look and laughed, lightly pushing my shoulder.

"You are such a perv."

I felt my eyebrows shoot up, "What? No- I'm not- no-" He chuckled again.

"Scarlett- I was just joking." I felt myself get angry at the embarrassment.

"Oh."

"Yeah," He laughed. He jutted his chin out the other way. "Come on." I glanced back at Bambi and her eyes were pleading from the doorway.

"Just one minute- I have to talk to Bambi about something." I jogged my way back to the door and she started speaking in a hushed tone.

"I told you that I don't like him, with you- you two together. I have a bad feeling and I don't like this one bit."

I leaned against the door frame, "I know I don't like this as much as you do, but it isn't fair that Hidalgo got time with me- and Hidalgo wasn't even the one who asked politely." She put a hand on her hip.

"He did *so* ask nicely- I have no idea what you mean."

I rolled my eyes at her. "Yeah, he sure asked nicely- someone who is yelling 'can I take her with me?' out the door as their dragging her away sure is *nicely asking*. Someone's got a boy crush much?"

"Someone has theirs?" She peeked around me at Romeo who was leaning against a tree, arms crossed, watching us. She turned back to me, and put her arms across her chest and raised her eyebrows.

I didn't understand at first- but then I got what she was saying. I gasped and felt my cheeks go red. "I *do not* like Romeo!" She smirked at me and shrugged.

"Yeah because all those loving looks, and the hand on the shoulder action *so* said how much you hate the boy. Puh-lease, Scarlett Todd- you're not pulling anything on me." She rolled her eyes.

"I am just trying to be fair."

"Oh ho ho, your 'trying to be fair', uh huh, right." Her voice went stupid and she crossed her eyes, trying to imitate me.

"You suck at that."

"Yeah I know- not the point thought- you're going to fall for that boy, just like I did with Jeffrey and then he will crush you long and hard- and you're not going to like it." I stood there, giving her a blank look so I didn't upset her, because she was a good friend, and she was telling me these things because she cared about me deeply. That was sweet and she deserved respect after the help and kindness she has given me.

"I will be cautious. I promise." She sighed and looked down at the ground, I just patted her shoulder. She smiled weakly at me.

"Fine. Go ahead." I smiled brightly at her.

"I promise."

"Okay." She smiled again and pushed me a little, "Now go- your *friend* is waiting for you." I scratched my head and patted her arm.

"I will be okay. Bye, I will come home at..."

"Seven."

"Okay, see you!" I ran back to Romeo and smiled, he smiled brightly too.

Once we were away out of hearing range, and Bambi closed her front door- he broke the silence between up with a curious, cocky grin.

"Talking shit?" He smiled and laughed kicking a rock to the side, as we walked our way somewhere.

"No, I just had to talk to her about some stuff like time, because I have plans tonight."

He laughed, his voice filled with beautiful volume, melodic deep tones erupting from his throat. "You just trying to get rid of me, Todd?" I smiled and pushed my falling glasses up my nose and pulled a bunch of my hair so that it was covering the shoulder facing him. I peeked out from behind my hair.

"No, I am *not*. I just....have plans." I kept watching forward and saw the most beautiful car ever to grace my eyes. I stopped right in my tracks and looked all around me to see no other cars in sight around it. "This can't be your car."

"And why not?" I glanced at him, wide eyed

"This isn't your car."

"Isn't it though?" He laughed, and scratched the back of his head, getting closer to me.

"You're *joking* right?" He smiled even brighter, and his eyes lit like a Christmas tree.

"This car? Here?" I rolled my eyes and pointed to it.

"Yes this car! *This car!*" He chuckled at me, and put his hand on the small of my back, leading me to the car.

"Scarlett, it's just a matte black Lamborghini Murcielago LP670-4 SV." He let go of me and hopped into the front seat, and waved me, mouth gaping, into the car.

"This can't be yours!" I yelled from the outside.

"It's wicked isn't it? That I have *this car*." He shook his head and yelled back at me, "Because you seem to have more interest in telling me that over and over instead of getting in here!" I laughed and ran to the car door and pulled up the door in awe.

I lightly sat inside and gaped some more at how cool it looked, with the black and bumblebee yellow leather interior. The car was heated up and ready for us to go.

"This is amazing! How the fuck did you get this?!" I rubbed the leather and looked at all the knobs and buttons, yellow and black.

"Bets. I am fucking amazing at pool, if you didn't know." He turned the key and the car started to purr. We were soon off, and he drove like a maniac.

I clutched the seat and sat far back in my seat, breathing really hard- I quickly pushed my glasses up, and clawed at the seat again. Romeo chuckled low at me and I could see he was starting to accelerate as he got more excited.

"Slow down! Now!" He threw his head back and started chuckling, letting the car swerve a little. "Romeo- now! Fucking slow down!" He shot me an amused look and raised his brows trying to hold in another giggle.

"Slow down? You want me to slow-" He shoved his foot down on the pedal and we quickly got faster, now on gravel roads leading into the countryside. "Down?" I felt my eyes widen, as I heard pebbles start to hit the back of the car.

"Fuck, Romeo! We're going to die!" I almost thought I heard him growl as he slid to a stop. Once we were going zero miles an hour and the car quieted to a slow purr again, he threw his head back and laughed- smacking both of his hands on the steering wheel. He abruptly stopped and swallowed glancing at me, seriously.

"Are you-" He giggled a little again, covering his mouth, "Okay, Scarlett?" He was left in a fit of giggles, trying his best not to laugh again. I clutched my chest and realized that I was hyperventilating. I slowed my breathing then punched his arm really hard, "Ow!"

"What the fuck?! You drive like a fucking maniac, you idiot! Did you want to get us killed?" He laughed again, and rubbed my shoulder- serious again, not laughing.

"No, I drive like that all the time Scarlett- I wasn't going to kill us, you scared cat." I inhaled and sunk down in my chair.

"I'm not a scared cat- you're just a shitty driver." He laughed again and leaned over me, slouching in the seat.

"Oh, so now I am a shitty driver, huh?" I laughed, completely sarcastic and rose in my seat again and punched him again in the shoulder- this time, a lot lighter.

"Yes, you're a fucking shitty driver- and I would never trust you to give *anyone*, including me, a ride." He frowned at me, playing.

"Meanie."

"Maniac." We both laughed and his hand reached for the key again. "Oh, dear lord." I braced myself for the crazy driving, and buckled my seat belt. "Bambi is going to be pissed at me for letting you kill me." He cracked up on me, and turned the engine off to my surprise.

"Get out, we're already here, you big goof." He opened both doors with a button and hopped out making me seem like an idiot just sitting there. I unbuckled my seat belt and got out as well, and looked around me, catching my surroundings. We were in the middle of nowhere and there was grass the height of my thigh everywhere, besides on the hill where there were only little patches of the tall grass.

"Uh, where are we?" He went around the back and popped the trunk, taking out a big duffel bag.

"No where." He smirked at me and started walking in the tall grass, stopping short of the bottom of the jut of grass popping out of the side of the road. "Well? Are you coming or what?" I raised my eyebrow to amuse him.

"I *guess*." I chased after him and laughed, as we made our way up the big hill-which took about twenty minutes. By the time we reached the top, there was a checkered blanket, with a guitar case laying on it, and it was *the* perfect view of a golden, magenta sunset. The sunset shaded Romeo's face with a salmon, golden light, his beautiful black eyes almost glittering off of the illuminated sky. He sat the duffel bag down and sat on the blanket, me following suit. I peered at the sunset, raising a hand in front of me so that I could see it better without the sun in my eyes, and examined the beautiful pink and orange ball that was half gone behind the other side of earth. I smiled, and took a deep breath. "This is...so beautiful."

"Yeah, I go here to play. And to get away from my mother." He chuckled and unzipped the duffel bag grabbing two ham sandwiches in two little baggies. I laughed when he pulled out about thirty little bottles of juice after that. I giggled and covered my mouth, giving him a questioning look. "You will get it later- were doing something else after this."

"Oh, okay." I took my sandwich out of my bag and took a bite, while he looked through all the different mixtures of juice and pulled two out that were the same color. He handed one to me and I smiled taking a sip. I felt my eyes bug out when the taste of the liquid hit my tongue. "Oh my god- did you make this?" He gave me a cautious look and slowly answered.

"Yeah...why?" I swallowed and set it down on the blanket, smiling at him brightly.

"Because that was the best juice drink I have ever tried- what did you mix together?" He chuckled at me and took his sandwich out.

"Okay so what I put in it was-" He then took a big bite out of his sandwich and started talking again, muffled out words, "Muff fa foo an bah mama poo fa foo!" I laughed and dipped my fingers in a little of my juice and flicked it at him. "*Bay!*" He rolled his eyes and swallowed the mouthful and started again, "Hey!"

"Meanie!" I started laughing again and he smirked.

"*I'm* the meanie? Who just flicked juice at my face?" I giggled and finished my sandwich while he did too. He put all the trash and the little bottles of juice, including my empty one, inside the duffel bag and opened the case and pulled out his guitar. His guitar was a beautiful cherry red, with a black pick looking thing piece attached onto it, probably for decoration. He put it in his lap and adjusted his arm so that he had his armpit in the crook of the side of the guitar. He started to pluck many high notes, up the fret board, and he intricately moved his fingers around, between and on certain strings. Then he started to sing and I found myself enticed and astonished.

"Life isn't hard with the lovely parts played,
Not only do I find clarity but I find heart payed,
And with this empty house and this empty mind,
Do I find the one and only that should be mine."

He paused and kept playing a little bit, and I found myself staring at his face, his eyes shut, instead of his fingers. He then kept singing, his voice a little low, and very high in some parts.

"Only do I see this barred person,
Whipped and carried beyond comparison,
In the mirror of my dismay,
and to these broken bones shall I pray."

He played more and more, and sang very beautifully until the end of the song, then opened his eyes and smiled a little then looked up to see me, head cocked, eyes wide, and smiling lightly at him.

"That was very beautiful." He smiled a little bigger at me, and pointed at me.

"Now it's your turn that you learned a little." My smiled vanished, and I felt a little afraid.

"There is no way that I can play like you did, I would be so bad at that. No, no I am perfectly fine sitting here- play more!" He chuckled and raised one eyebrow at me.

"No, no you are learning- you're not getting out of this by flattery. Come on," He pulled a little on my arm, with a gentle smiled and I sighed and scoot to where he was sitting, when he stood up for me to sit down. I sat there and Romeo just stood behind me. "Move up a little." I scoot over the left and he shook his head, "No, *up*."

"Oh," I scoot back to where I was but this time, I moved forward in front of me.

"Good." He sat the guitar down next to me. "Now hold the guitar like I was." I curled my fingers around the fret board and lightly set them down on the strings, while my other hand hung over the side. "Okay, now here." I heard him shuffle from behind me and then felt his hands on my sides and he knelt down to where he sat on his calves, knees locked around my waist. He took his hands off my sides and I could feel his breath on my neck as his head popped up on the side of mine, and his arms curled around mine- adjusting my arm correctly so I had the side of the guitar snug in my armpit. He took my right hand and curled his other hand around my left hand, his fingers set over mine. I felt his hair tickle my ears, and his breath tickle my neck as he fully bent around my whole body. I felt my hips and legs tense because I wasn't all that comfortable with him being so close to me.

"Okay, now relax your hands for a moment- you're clawing at the wood around the strings." He slipped his fingers in between my left hand's fingers and made my hand let go the stings and the board, and he enveloped his left hand around mine, holding it there. "Just relax." I felt my fist, which was in his hand- relax and I looked up at him. "Good." He said.

He made me uncurl my fingers from the fist and laid them back on the fret board. "I don't think this is a good idea." I felt my throat go dry and I coughed.

"Don't worry, you will be just fine playing," He chuckled and bent over a little more so that his chin was lying on my shoulder. That wasn't what I meant when I said it, but I let it go anyways. "Now put you fingers-" He grabbed my pointer finger, my middle finger, and my ring finger and put them in a staircase line on the strings and then lightly pushed down. "Like that, and then pushed down so that you have a firm down hold on the strings." I pressed a little harder and swallowed, getting hot from the sunset's rays on us. "Good, now-" Then he took my wrist on my right hand and gently started strumming, a pretty and gentle note coming out from the strings. I started to strum on my own and soon he let go of both of my hands and sat in front of me, while I was smiling and strumming. I closed my eyes like he did, and found myself plucking beautifully. I felt myself get dizzy then I was reeling back, a flashback coming back to me. Everything was black, and I had no consciousness of what I was doing, then a deep, deep memory from the complete back of my mind fuzzed into view, and soon everything around me changing.

# Chapter 25

Once I was done reeling back into my thoughts, I was fully living back a memory. "Heth, teach me the words on the thin notes, the beauty that is in strings!" He reached out from behind the guitar and smashed his finger onto my lips.

"Shh! Valetta, they shall be soft-spoken or they heed find us, and hear our melodic tones!" He chuckled lowly, I looked down with tears in my eyes, feeling offended even though I shouldn't have. His grin turned into a frown and he grabbed my chin so that I would look at him instead of the hay that was under us that I was running my hand over, "I didn't intend to emotionally wound you, you needn't cry, Valetta." I felt a tear run down my cheek.

"No good is done when the one to open up isn't forsaken, as well until her death. The death of me should be these barrels and these jagged wood shreds, in which the boy I sit with will hypnotize thee to no end. He shall have given me my faith, and my sins- making me a sinning wench!" I stood up, ripping my chin out of his soft grip. I ran to the barn door and ran out, running in the field until Heth came from behind me and took my shoulders, spinning me around until I was close in his arms. His voice lowered to a whisper.

"You never shall be a wench, nor forsaken- only ones who cherish thy black hair and tanned cheeks will only bring till your death- nor will you be killed by the unworthy hell barren man that you call a *father*." He spat the other way and pain held in his slate grey eyes. His arms pleading for my embrace in return, his face pleading for me to listen closely.

"Please, come- come with me, be with me, please Valetta, be my holy maiden, I would never treat you as would he- thy love for you is too saintly to make me sin against you or with you until wiven." I pulled away from his embrace and stared into those sparkling grey eyes, seeing years and years of wisdom even though we were young.

"I needn't want the lashes and pain if caught- and scolded. Branding is my punishment for not sweeping the floors as correct and requested as done. I fear-"

"You fear prosperous light and swiftly ways! Free will and bare opportunities, thy darkest ways of being unchained-" I yanked out of his grip and started walking away, but he kept jogging behind me.

"Unchained be not my fear as well as the *pain* and the *suffering* that I will have to pay- due to *your matter!*" He ran in front of me, us both yelling at each other because we were a couple miles from the barn and the house- not realizing she walked so far, I abruptly stopped when Heth stepped in front of me, blocking my path.

"Not thy matter- but of the matter of *love!*" He fell to his knees in front of me, grabbing my hands. I stood there quiet, watching him, looking down on this crying man that knelt in front of me on the grass. He took a minute to gain his bearings and then started again, quieter. "Heed my callings to you, Valetta, as you watch a broken man plead. Not only is thy *soul* in this, by the name known as deep love, but is my broken *being* in this as well. Not my mind that speaks to me, nor my heart- but my *soul*. Thy love is just so hard handled that you can't strip the layers of my cold shriveled heart and take thy feelings, then go take what you make of them. Thy do not *know* the things that thee would do for thee- may it be risk my life and be dropped as a frigid corpse, or sell my soul to the devil- you *are* what I need."

I felt my heart crush at his words, apparently to his words- I was all he had to care about in this life. I cared deeply about Heth too though, because I have fallen in love with him. But I also cared about my life, and if I was caught- I would surely be murdered by my father or his watchmen. Trust me, I wanted to die- but not by them.

"Your heeded pleas crackle my heart. Though thy can not find a way to break the steel chains that *do* lay with me. I love thee more than the star bursts can break. Forgive me, but my death lay not with my age but with my father. Thy can not find a way to swim through truth, free, and not be followed. Fear would be our mother, and hell would be our home."

I bent down on my knees and took his face into my hands, and stared into those beautiful eyes.

"Thy can not find a way to trust? Thy can not break free? Protector and knight's wind would guide you, as I am your savior." His tears dried by now, and his face was left blotchy and red. He swiftly slipped his hands on my cheeks- intertwining with my hair. The only thing I could hear was our heavy breathing, as he watched my hair while he ran his fingers through it- down my back. Once he was embracing me again, his face got close to mine and we put our foreheads together. "Run away with me." I inhaled his minty breath and closed my eyes and shivered.

"Don't, please." I started to quietly sob, sitting there in his arms with him, our foreheads pressed together. He started crying as well, silent. I felt him shiver as he tilted his head a little to the side, our tears dancing with each other- becoming one.

"I love you, Valetta."

"I love you too, Heth." I let out one last cry before he fell into me, kissing me. I lay on the ground, as he held up his own weight so he wouldn't lie on top of me. I sat up and moved the hair out of his eyes, my eyes shut all the while. Once he pulled away, we both put our foreheads back together, both of our expressions broken and pained, as we cried.

He clutched a clump of my hair in one hand and his other hand was on my neck, as both of my hands lay lightly on his shoulders. He again said, "Run away with me."

I took a deep breath and swallowed, shaking all over. "Oh....Okay." My eyes slowly opened, and I saw his smile, elated. His eyes shot open and he was crying, smiling.

"Valetta!" I smiled and he jumped on top of me, I laughed a little and he kissed me deeply. He pulled away and he took my hand, kissing the palm and worked his way up my arm until he got to my shoulder- then kissed me again one more time on the lips.

77

"Thy love be so gentle but so deep that thy maiden cannot regret it, comes from the angels lips is the holy words of my heaven." I laughed once and he wiped a tear from my cheek.

"Only if thee waits till dawn of the day morrow. Then...thy must meet with you again to seek the lines of freedom and soon after escape- we *will* be wiven."

"Counting the seconds." He smiled and wiped away his tears of joy. "Now go, thee must be resting for our humble journey. I love you, Valetta." He kissed my cheek and ran off in the other directing, while I sit there on the grass and look back at the little dot of a red barn. Then everything went black.

When I opened my eyes, and plucked the last note- I set the guitar down and peered up at Romeo, who in fact- had his eyes bugged out, his mouth handing wide open, and his whole body slumped. We both were silent for a moment- and he remained the way he was sitting. Then he broke the silence, *"Holy shit, Scarlett!"*

I laughed nervously, having no knowledge of what I even played.

"You just played a Dave Matthews Song!" He sat up strait and kept his eyes shooting from the guitar and back at me.

"Who's he?" His mouth, that closed after speaking fell again and his head dropped.

"What the fuck do you mean 'who is he'?! You just played on of his songs just now!" He grabbed his head freaking out, "You just serious- w-what?!" He grabbed the guitar and looked at it, then at my hands. He sat back on his knees "You just played a twelve-string song, with a six string guitar, Scarlett! That's literally impossible!" He kept stumbling over his own words, "H-how did you *do* that?!"

"I- I don't know! I have no idea what you're talking about! I literally don't remember playing! My mind went blank and everything was black the whole time!" He laughed without humor.

"There is *no way* that you don't remember playing that or singing that!" I nodded frantically and put my hand to my heart.

"I swear to god! If you hand me the guitar now, I won't remember how to play a thing!"

"Pfft! Yeah right!" He jerked the guitar at me and I grabbed it and thought for a moment. My mind came up blank on how to play besides that one note he showed me.

"Uh..."

"Your joking right?!" I looked back up at him and shook my head.

"Whatever- I know I am not crazy!" I sighed and he looked at the sunset that darkened a little because it fell a tiny bit lower. I had no knowledge of this Dave Matthews, but I knew that when I get the chance I will have to listen to his music.

# Chapter 26

I didn't remember that we were supposed to do two things until I pondered on what he was saying before.

"Hey what was that other thing we were going to do?" He looked at the duffel bag.

"Oh yeah. Come on," He put the guitar back in its case, grabbed the duffel bag and stood up. I looked back down at the guitar case.

"Aren't you going to take that along? In case it rains or something?" He glanced down at the guitar and back up at the sunset.

"Nah, that would be stealing." He tore his eyes off the sun and looked at me.

"Huh?" He laughed and pointed at the guitar.

"Oh, that? Yeah, that guitar isn't mine." I felt my eyes go wide and my jaw tense.

"What?!"

He laughed again, "Yeah some stupid guy left it here for the past month, I have just been playing it every other day that I come here. I found it awhile ago, and so far they haven't come back for it."

"Oh..."

"Yeah." He went over the edge of the hill and I ran after him, smiling slightly. When we came over the hill- I saw a big stand with a huge white wall leaning against it, and a white tarp on the bottom. Then there was a camera set up there too.

"Is the camera yours at least?" He just chuckled at me, shook his head in amusement and ran down the hill. That didn't technically count as an answer but I let it go anyways. He laughed, happy in his step as he ran down the hill as fast as he could. I ran after him barefoot, carrying my shoes, and giggled as we raced down the hill. We both ran as fast as we could, rocketing towards the board, then we both smacked it at the same time- causing the board to slowly tip over from our impact.

"Oh shit!" He laughed, and we went headfirst onto the ground, the white wall landing on top of us. We both laughed and rolled out from under it, perching it up back against the big stand- which we had to put back together. He clapped his hands back together and sighed, with a big smile on his face. "So! For this part of the outing, we are going to be playing this sort of...game thing." Almost as if it was impossible- he grinned bigger. He got in the duffel bag and pulled out all the juice mixes and then pulled out a blindingly white bikini, then pulled out another blindingly white swimsuit for him, which were swim trunks.

"Er, I am not really a swim suit kind of girl..." He walked over and handed me the bikini then raised his eyebrow and chuckled at me, pushing my shoulder a little.

"You've got nothing to hide, do you?" His smile, his teeth were about as white as the bikini in my hand. His teeth also were extremely strait.

"No, I *don't*." I spun around, looking all around me. "Where can I change?" He squinted and looked around as well.

"Well, guess you'll just have to strip behind the wall." He smirked devilishly and my eyes went wide.

"But what if someone sees me?!" He chuckled and walked backwards toward the wall.

"Well, I guess they get a free peek then." He winked at me and popped behind the wall. I started walking around the corner, until I saw his jeans and boxers fly through the air and land in front of me. I jumped back from them like they were a nuclear bomb, and spun around from the side of the board and covered my eyes, even though I was turned.

"Are you *undressing* back there?" I felt myself move the hair behind my ears, nervous.

"Do you see any trees anywhere? Of course I am undressing back here!" He laughed sarcastically. "I mean, unless you want me to out there?" I felt my mouth drop open.

"*No!*" I practically screamed at the top of my lungs- he just chuckled from behind the white board. I heard the crunch of the grass under him as he stepped out from behind to board behind me. "Please tell me that you're not standing behind me, nude." He laughed.

"Well you will just have to look and see now don't you?" I stood there, turned away from him, silent, covering my eyes. "Either you do that- or you will have to find out by me doing a whole body tangle hug. You choose." I sighed and turned around, with a strong hold grip on my face still, and slowly moved my hand down my face. Neck...bare chest...V line... white shorts. Thank god.

"He laughed- now wasn't that so hard? You go change now." I laughed without humor at him, and he stuck his fists on the sides of his body like superman. "Will I have to carry you there and-"

"I'm going! I'm going! God!" I ran behind the wall, and looked at the bikini, which in fact had thin fabric and no bra padding. "You picked *this certain swimsuit* just for me didn't you, Romeo?" I heard him chuckle darkly.

"Well of course I did- its fit *just for you!*" I stood there for a moment, and nodded my head and glared at the wall.

"More fit for a porn star than for me..." He cleared his throat innocently.

"Oh, what's that, Scarlett?"

"Nothing!" He chuckled some more and I flicked him off from the other side of the wall. "No peeking!"

He just kept chuckling, "Oh, no- I would never do that! You know me!" I shook my head and stripped as fast as I could, slipping the swimsuit over my bra and underwear, then took off my bra and underwear so that if I *was* being watched, nothing scandalous showed.

When I walked out from behind the board, Romeo was turned away from me, bent over, messing around with some grass. His swimsuit fell low on his waist and he had a full fledged tattoo of big black wings across his back. *Sweet Jesus.*

"Oh...*my god.*" I felt my finger linger on my bottom lip, as I stared. He turned around himself and stared back at me too.

"Oh *my* god." We both stood there, in an awkward electrified silence- just shamelessly staring at each other's bodies. I was the one to break the silence and keep on track.

"What are we doing for this activity." He snapped out of his trance and shook his head, scratching his scalp.

"Uh, well- see those juice containers? Well *in* them are special food coloring dye that affects clothing, especially *white, new* clothing." He glanced down at the juice and back at me smiling.

I didn't know where he was getting at, at all so I just shook my head, swaying my hands, and narrowing my eyes. "*And?*" His smile turned wickedly devilish on me, as he picked up a juice cup and took as leisurely sip.

"So..." He picked up another cup, along with the one he was holding and raised his eyebrows. "This means that we're going to have a juice fight, in order to make our own swimsuits." He took two long strides toward me and teasingly tipped the glasses so that they almost spilled on me. "Move and it goes down Scarlett." He cocked his head and my body went still. He wrapped his arms around my neck and his husky voice whispered into my ear. "Sike!" I felt my eyes grow wide as then he poured the juice in the back of my swimsuit bottoms.

"Your going to *die!*" I growled as we both went darting toward the cups, running from each other, grabbing as many cups as we could possibly carry. I chucked a bluish-green one at him, and he ducked, but since he forgot about gravity, the cup smacked right on his back, pouring down into his trunks.

"Oh, that is it!" He ran over to me, pinned me face down to the ground and poured about five cups of juice all over my back and butt, then the last cup in his arms- right on my head.

"Get the hell off of me so I can kill you, you jerk!" Romeo lightly kept me pushed to the ground, not to the point where he could hurt me, but enough so that I wasn't able to get up.

"Oh really? What are you going to do about it?" I heard myself groan from his weight on my back, it was time for him to get off of me, and get off of me now. So I turned my ankle so it stretched a little bit, aimed strait back then swung my heel as long and hard as I could right into the arch of the spine of his back. He cried in pain, and fell over prolonging time for me to grab a couple more cups then straddle him so he couldn't get up.

81

Sitting on his tummy, I smirked at the man that I was sitting on in front of me, with his face screwed up in a mixture of pain, confusion and dark humor. "That was what I did about it." He sighed and I took a cup of reddish purple juice that smelt of cranberries and plums, and dumped it right on his face. He scrunched up his face, blowing out his nose so he didn't snuff it up, then licked his lips and smiled.

"Yum passion fruit- my favorite." I laughed and he grabbed my hips, throwing me off of him then made a mad dash towards the cups and grabbed a couple, while I had enough time to scramble up off the ground and run the opposite direction. We ran in circles around the white wall and then on my way back around while he was trying not to spill the contents of the cup on the ground, I grabbed one and chucked it at him. From the luck I had it landed smack dab on his thigh letting a huge blue stain start to migrate down the white fabric of his left leg.

"Your gonna get it Scarlett!" He curled his arm in and chucked a cup at me with perfect aim and strength before I could turn the corner, and it landed right on my chest- a big pink blotch on the left of my right breast. Thankfully he didn't hit it right on otherwise that would have sucked.

I ran from the right and he ran from the left- both of us sprinting as fast as we could toward the cups, but we slid from the juice that soaked in the grass, and both of us ran into each other landing on all of the cups- then making us both soaked in a fruity kitty pool. We both scrambled to grab cups and pour what was left of them on each other, laughing up a storm. Once we were sure all of the cups were empty, we lay on crumpled plastic, little jagged points from the cups stabbing into our backs, laughing and catching our breath. It soon got quiet.

"That was fun."

"Yeah." We both started chuckling again and he stood up, holding out a hand to help me up. I took it knowing if I tried being independent, I would slip and fall on my butt...like every other time. I graciously took it, and in response he smirked from the minor ego pump. Typical Romeo.

# Chapter 27

"Okay, since we're done with that- what is the big board for?" He smiled at me, his fang teeth almost glittering against the striking sun. He ran down a little dip in the hill couple yards away, and I waited as he soon came back carrying bucket after bucket of paint. He set all the pints of colors around us, and he grabbed my hand and pulled me on the tarp in front of the camera.

"Think of this as our 'first date' shot, babe- smile!" I rolled my eyes, and smiled as he clicked the button, and we both leaned into the camera- one arm around each of our necks. Just before it flashed, he planted a big kiss on my cheek and I could feel the smile in his lips. Once the flash blinded me- I blinked a few times as I sat back up, irritated. He pulled the picture out of the Polaroid Camera. I walked over to him and looked over his shoulder as it started to color into view.

When I saw the picture, I can honestly say, I went a little speechless.

"Don't we look so... *adorable?*" He chuckled and handed me the picture for me to see myself, and I felt my mouth open lightly- silently gaping at the image of us.

In the picture, we were both leaning towards the camera, me smiling like I won the lottery while he kissed me on the cheek, his dimples on his cheeks bones showing as his teeth showed the white smile as his lips were pressed against my cheek, we both had big, wet, frizzy hair and since we were standing in front of the white wall, the flash made it look like we had a white cloud around us, then behind that board was the most beautiful pinkish-orange half sun, with sun rays shooting everywhere, varying from reds to deep yellows. It was very cute and surprisingly it made pink spread to my cheeks lightly as well. I closed my mouth quickly and shoved my arm in his direction.

"Yeah, cute." I said a little hostile. I didn't want to admit that I thought it was amazing. It wasn't amazing, he wasn't amazing- we weren't amazing. We are... acquaintances, and I needed to rap my brain around that idea.

"Wait! I have a finishing touch to the picture!" He ran over to his bag, pulled out a red permanent marker, and scribbled the two words 'first date' on the bottom, then a bunch of perfect red hearts around it and filled in the hearts. I didn't stop him because I knew that if he already wrote it, he might as well finish it.

He held it out in front of him to admire his artwork and grinned. "I don't know about you but I like this photo." I rolled my eyes again and turned to the white wall, holding my arms. I watched the endless sunset feeling a sense of déjà vu as I wondered if it would ever just *go down* already.

He came from behind me and stood beside me, "The paint is so that we can create a big mural on that wall." He plucked a screw driver out of the bag and I felt my eyes twitch and grow a little bigger as it reminded me of Mary Poppin's Purse. How did he *fit* everything in there? He grabbed a can and pried it open as a nice salmon pink puddle showed itself from the inside, and the more I glanced down at it- the more I noticed several tones from the sunset matched it.

"Cool." He nodded as he threw me another screw driver, an orange handled one, that I hadn't seen him grab when he took the first one out. I grabbed a mystery can and easily popped it open as a vibrant cerulean blue came into view. I smiled on the inside as it was one of my favorite colors. I looked over at Romeo who stumped my rate of two cans open by the time of two minutes, by his six. His face was screwed up in concentration as he cracked them open at a fast rate. I grabbed another can and opened it with a little struggle to see a nice bright orange come into view.

By the time we were finished, my seven compared to his seventeen, we both stood up and stepped back to evaluate our handy work of opening them all.

"They did it perfect. Twenty-four cans- all the colors in a pack of twenty-four crayons, just like I asked," I looked up at him, he was nodding in appreciation, "I am impressed."

"You asked for all the colors in a pack of crayons?" I chuckled a little at his childishness.

"A pack of crayons and my guitar are the only friends I had growing up you know." He smirked at me and I felt a little guilty for making-fun.

"I'm so-" He shook me off, shaking his head.

"Don't say sorry, it was my childhood and I am already over it." I sensed a tad bit of snootiness in his voice, probably from me hitting a nerve that he didn't want to be brought up again.

"Fine then." He pulled out four cardboard boards and lay on top of it, creating a pose, and by this point I didn't ask anymore because everything was pretty predictable.

"Trace me." He said simply, tossing the red marker my way. I did as I was told and once I was finished, he got up and made me lay down. "Make whatever cool or funny pose you want." I made a disco pose with one hand in the air and the other pointing towards the floor, then after that he traced me and I stood up again, him lying on another board making another pose, I traced him without a word. Once I was done tracing him again, I lay on the last board and made a pose as if I was jumping, and made two peace signs in the air too. We then cut them out and once we were finished we pulled back to see all the pose cuts we had.

There was a disco pose and a jumping peace sign pose, mine, then there was a superman pose with hands on his hips, looking up and there was also a pose with a guy holding his muscularly arms up, Romeo's. I saw Romeo slowly grin from the corner of my eye, and then he picked up a roll of duct tape laying on the ground and pulled a big strip out then stuck the two ends together, flipping the board over and smacking it to the back.

Silently I did what he was doing then once tape was securely on the back of all the cut outs, I smiled at him. "What now?" I almost thought my voice echoed after all the silence we just experienced. I also think he jumped when I said that.

"Now what we do, is we smack these cut outs on the board but make the cut outs, at least a foot off the ground and make them at least a foot and a half apart." He glanced at me and smiled. "Okay?" I just grinned back.

"Gotcha champ." I laughed "How about we make it like boy-girl, boy-girl so that it looks a little cooler?" He nodded after looking at the wall one more time.

"Yeah that would work good. Let's do it!" We both chuckled and grabbed them, sticking them in the order I suggested. The pose order that it ended up being was my disco one, his muscle one, my jumping one, then his superman one. "Okay, now here's where the fun part comes in. Both of us either take a cup or a brush, and then we just *fling* paint at the wall! You think you can do that?" I has this big cheesy grin on my face just thinking about it.

"Fuck yeah I think I can!" I ran and grabbed a brush then grabbed the pinkish salmon looking one on the can reading the name. "I think I will go with good old *cranberry* here." He giggled and I set the can down toward the tarp on the ground. I slowly dipped my brush in getting a good amount sopping up my brush, then slung it towards the board, watching as the bubbles of paint spewed onto the white wall, in slow motion as they splattered. I grabbed a cup off of the ground and threw it to him as I sloshed some more *cranberries* onto the wall. I smiled brightly as we went straight for the black can.

"Typical Romeo... always hyping up his persona." He rolled his eyes at me and smirked.

"Yeah? What about Miss Scarlett? Boys always draping all over her?" I felt a red flag fly up in my head.

"Excuse me? Who is draping over *me*? Mister Nina butt rubber?" I saw his eyes go wide, as he flung a glopping cup of paint at the wall.

"Excuse *me*? *That* was dancing! And what do you mean 'who is draping over me?'- you pretty much have *everyone* ogling you Scarlett!"

"Uh huh- dancing...right." I smirked myself and rolled my eyes slouching my way over to a blue can of paint. "And what do you mean *ogling*. No one is *ogling* me- I don't know what you mean by that. The only person who would probably be ogling me is *you*, because that's what you do with every other girl I have ever seen in eternity." He grabbed an orange paint can and ladled out the paint in his cup and threw it at the wall, his chuckled darkly.

"Yeah, right, Scarlett. I love to eye fuck you and everything. Your dreaming."

"Uh huh, right." I rolled my eyes for what seemed like the fifth time in the last five minutes. He did hang over me a little bit but not all the time, but I still didn't get what he meant by everyone 'draping over me'. That just didn't make sense at all. It was silent for a couple minutes but I felt what he said eating at me. By the time I had at least six colors of my doing on the wall, I made my way over to a purple can. "Guys do not drape over me, I don't know what you're talking about."

He just chuckled, "It really bugs you to know that every man you pass on the street stares at you, doesn't it?" He sloshed his red cup of paint at the wall, and I took a sling myself.

"Yes, to be honest. Its sleazy and disgusting to me to have men staring at me all the time. I don't take that as a compliment fully." He tightened his strong, pale jaw, and carefully pushed his hair behind his ear. I couldn't happen but notice as he was leaning down that his tattoo of black wings, stretched, almost like they would curl around you.

"I don't know why guys do it, you're just pretty so they look. Simple explanation." He sighed, and I could hear irritation trickling into his voice slowly as the conversation about me prolonged.

"Well I know but, how can I make them stop?" I kept glancing at him between throwing paint and noticed he refused to look at me. He face screwed up in annoyance.

"I don't know- wear a ski mask? How the hell should I know?" I pursed my lips and went for a yellow can.

"Well... I mean,"

"I just don't know- okay? Seriously, I have no idea how to make guys stop looking at you. You're going to have to get over it that your averagely pretty. Most girls would want to be like you." His jaw was tensing and un-tensing the point where I thought it was pulsating.

I felt the need to ask what was wrong, but didn't want to push his buttons. He grabbed my arm and pulled me a little closer to him, looking into my eyes deeply. I saw his Adam's apple bob as he swallowed dryly.

"I think it's done." When I looked over, he took off the cut outs and it looks like a big beautiful colorful mess.

"I think we did amazing." I landed my gaze back on him and he was just about to open his mouth to say something when his phone buzzed on the floor next to us.

He didn't pull his gaze off of me though, he swiftly picked it up and flicked it open, putting it up to his ear. I heard a muffled out voice on the end and his blank face slowly turned into a devilish smile. "We'll be there." He answered, and then snapped it shut again.

"Where are we going?" His smirk got bigger.

"Do you ever go partying?"

The last time I went to a party...it wasn't one of my favorite memories. But I was still curious on what he was thinking. "Yes." I answered slowly. "Why?"

"Scarlett, I am going to show you one hell of a time."

# Chapter 28

He didn't tell me where we were going. I questioned him the whole time- while we were cleaning up, while we were gathering our belongings, while we were bunching the paint cans- the whole process was me non-stop babbling. The only question he answered was when I asked about the canvas and leaving it there, and his only response was, "Someone will come to pick it up later."

He was smiling the whole time that we were cleaning up and it was scaring me. He was smiling on the way back to the car, he was smiling while loading up the trunk, and he was smiling while I called Bambi telling her I would be a little later, (which by the way she wasn't too happy about). He was just...smiling. Mischievously. And it was seriously frightening me.

"Where are we going?" I started to feel the panic sink in when it was pitch black and we were driving through and alley.

"Have you ever heard of underground parties?" I raised my eyebrows and then felt really shocked.

"*What?!*" I leaned forward in my chair and winced as the seat belt rubbed my neckline red.

"You know, parties? Underground?" He seriously thought I didn't understand what those were.

"Yes, I have heard of underground parties you fucking fuck ass!" He raised his eyebrows in amusement.

"Really? What a comeback. Anyways, my friend Louche is throwing a party, and I want to warn you now- don't take the drugs. They're not clean." I felt my eyes grow about five times bigger.

"Excuse me?! Drugs? Get me out of this fucking car now!"

"Jump out if you want." He sped up the car so that we were going twenty over the limit.

"Slow down! Now!" He smirked at me, his black hair falling into his face, his forearm muscles tensing and his fingers curling around the steering wheel.

"Jump if you'd like, I really wouldn't mind the lack of whining Scarlett!" He sped up more and I felt myself grip my seat harder.

"Fine! No questions asked. Just take me to the fucking party." We slowed down to a crawl. His grip on the wheel loosened, and he chuckled darkly.

"Doesn't matter. We're here. And like I said, no drugs. I don't want to take you home totally buzzed and possibly dying." He popped open our doors and I stepped out, as he threw a red t-shirt at me. "Cover your boobs a little. Curious hands are groping hands."

I slipped it over my head and put on my shoes. I felt the ground beneath me vibrate from all the base, and I was almost positive I saw the pebbles on the gravelly side of the road bounce. He opened what looked like a sewer door, but when I looked down I saw people jumping, people fist-pumping, people swaying, and people hopping their way through the crowd, all illuminated by strobe lights.

"Climb down." I did as he said, pushing up my glasses before making my way down the ladder. My hair was a frizzy mess and I had to make sure I stepped on the ladder steps instead of slipping on my hair.

When I stepped down into the cave looking, underground area- I instantly felt the humidity of all the body heat slap me in the face. It was fucking hot, and everyone around me was sweating. I already felt my heart start pumping hard and fast with the base of really good music that was playing all around me. Fumes of marijuana, cigarettes, alcohol and sweat filled my nose and I almost felt suffocated.

I jumped when Romeo's hand sat itself on my shoulder, and his smile that was all over his body as he pushed my hair back to yell in my ear. I could barely hear him, but his breathy, husky made its own white noise. I could barely make out, "What do you think?!" I took in my surroundings again and smiled at him, wobbling my hand back side to side. He let out a hearty laugh and hugged me, yelling again into my ear. "Lets go by... speakers- that's...where the most...fun..." I scrunched up my face and he shoved craned his face more into my ear. "Lets go by the speakers- that's where the most fun is!" I nodded and noticed his nice cotton pants that switched out the trunks, which in fact- I didn't see him put on. His hair was disheveled and he grabbed my hand and yanked me through the crowd. The music got louder and loud as we gained closer distance between the speakers and us, eventually it got so loud I thought it was going to bust my eardrums- but Romeo and the people around me didn't care.

Romeo bumped into someone and they started smiling and yelling a conversation to each other. Romeo tapped my shoulder and yelled to me, "This is Louche!" I put my eyes on the man before me.

He had dirty blond hair and was wearing an unbuttoned white dress shirt and dark wash jeans. His hair was all messed up, and his beautiful tan wash board abs were glowing in the strobe lights as he took a swig of a vodka bottle in his hand, already half gone. He took a couple steps toward me and pushed back the hair behind my ear so I could hear him. "Hello, darling, how do you like the party?" His English accent flowed into my hearing range. He said it, but it came out a little more like this. "Hello, dah-ling, how aw you liking the pah-tee?" I smiled and yelled into his ear.

"Its awesome, you throw amazing parties!" He pulled back and did a swift up and down sweep with his eyes over me and smiled brightly.

"I'm glad you like it, those amateur, mingling collage parties don't compare to the ones I make happen!" I pulled back and nodded, excited from all the music pulsing around me.

"Who is this playing?" I yelled to Romeo, he just shook his head and shrugged his shoulders, as Louche yelled into my ear.

"Its Passion Pit!"

"I have never heard of them!" He smirked, surprisingly seeming to have more ego than Romeo.

"Most haven't!" I nodded and went over to Romeo and slid my arm around his waist, not feeling physically comfortable with the suggestive stance that Louche was sending towards me. Romeo just slid a protective arm over my shoulders and pulled me close, my face coming in contact with the sweat already beading over his chest. It was a little nasty, but I got over it.

"Lets go dance!" Romeo nodded in question and I nodded back, smiling. We tugged our way into the crowd and Romeo started to sway back and forth, shaking his body back and forth rapidly. I started jumping up and down, raising my arms above my head getting into it. The whole crowd was jumping to the beat and every punch of the base that erupted from the speakers, all of us would land on the ground, a perfect wave of movement. My shirt was soaked from all the sweat, and my sticky skin from the delicious juice that was still deep in my pores didn't help my disgusting body either. But I didn't care- I just wanted to dance all my stresses away. Some people were grinding against each other and I came a little closer to Romeo, yelling out the words with the rest of the crowd, remember the words of the chorus. We both screamed our hearts out to the song in unison with the people around us and the music. When I looked at his face as he was yelling the lyrics, his face seemed almost pained as he closed his eyes and jumped along with me. His side swept bands were starting to frizz at the ends from his sweat, and his chest was dripping with colorful sweat- mostly from the juice dyes adding color. He smiled when he opened his eyes and saw me and grabbed hold of my waist, hoisting me up so that he was holding me on his front like a toddler. I threw my head back and chuckled as he jumped with the crowd still, my weight not making him miss a beat, and spun me around. I saw some other girls and guys on each other's shoulders out in the ocean of people, dancing along with the person who's shoulders that they were sitting on were.

I felt like I never wanted to leave, and everyone was smiling and laughing. The energy there was intoxicating a long with the smell of the drugs. Romeo put me back down on the ground and we started bouncing again as the chorus came up again.

"What song is this?" I yelled to him, giggling like crazy, out of breath. He smiling brightly at me and got closer to me so I could hear.

"Judging from the chorus- it might be called 'sleepyhead'?" I laughed and screamed with my arms above my head, and the crowd followed with a yell of their own. I blushed and looked all around me as everyone was bobbing their heads and jumping giving me high-fives. Romeo grabbed my hands and intertwined his fingers in with mine, he then spun me around and then I hopped on his back so he piggybacked me back to around where the speakers, which by the way was where everything was provided.

By everything, I mean drugs, alcohol and food.

He set me down and gestured that he would be right back, I nodded and looked at the table- averting my eyes from the drugs. I grabbed spiked lemonade and then scanned the food, my eyes catching on a tray of brownies which tons and ton of people were digging into. I grabbed one, shyly, and then took a bite out of it.

*My god.* The brownies were the best I have ever tasted in the history of baking. I ate the rest and looked back over to the tray to grab another and was bummed to see that all of them were gone already. I took a swig of my fruity drink with the vodka after taste setting in deep. I set the drink back down on the table and everything blurred a little bit. I looked in the crowd to find Romeo, and then spotted him and Louche eyeing me up and down. Romeo said something softly and Louche laughed and patted him on the back. Romeo smiled and slipped his way through the crowd without effort.

Once he got closer to me he smiled brightly, biting his tongue in a smile- which by the way was still pierced. "You loving the party, Scarlett?" I pulled his head close and spoke into his ear.

"Why wouldn't I this is fun- I love all these changing colored lights, you know." I giggled and felt my knees buckle, he caught me in time and watched me down seriously.

"Scarlett, there are no 'colored' lights." He looked me up and down again, but not flirtatiously this time. "Scarlett, did you take something?" I giggled again, sloppily rapping my arms around his neck and pressed my cheek onto his chest.

"Oh my god, Romeo, your t-shirt is so soft." I ran my hands all over the top half of his body and he grabbed my wrist, pulling me away from him so that he could look me in the eyes.

"Fuck, Scarlett- Focus. *What* did you take?!" I felt another fit of giggled erupt from me as I slid out of his arms and sat cross legged on the floor.

"I just ate food and took a drink of some... I don't fucking know- drink." he left me there for a moment while I saw him hazily run off in the other direction toward the tables. He spoke to a man with a joint between two fingers, serious faced. He ran back and picked me up, my whole body feeling ticklish and jelly. The room was spinning and when I grabbed his head and pulled him close to kiss him, he looked into my eyes with a look of what seemed like...he was ashamed.

Once my lips touched his, he dropped me so that I could stand, I rapped my arms tightly around his neck and I pressed my body as hard to his as possible. I could feel his screwed up expression relax and he grabbed my hips as I jumped onto him, my legs clinging around his waist. A new song was playing and blasting through my ears, 'New Perspective' by a band called 'Panic! At The Disco'. His whole body that was tense relaxed almost immediately. He slid his hands up my back and grabbed my hair, pulling a little at the deep roots on my head. I tilted my head, tasting a bright smile on his lips. I peeked at him a little to see his eyes go from wide to clamping them shut. I squeezed my eyes shut and got closer. I needed closer, I wanted closer- this felt right, I needed him. All of him, right now, right here.

After a little bit, I pulled away slowly and it was almost like it was in slow motion. He stared wide eyed at me, until I saw a small grin fall onto his lips. I smiled brightly and smashed my lips back onto his. I pulled on the hair that was in my hands behind his neck, and I felt my insides go on fire. I pulled myself pull away again, his white smile and twinkling eyes grinning at me as well as I whispered some of the lyrics in his ear, "*I wanna live my life from a new perspective.*" He laughed and kissed me a couple more times. I felt myself drifting away from the light and I laid my head onto his shoulder, falling asleep in his arms like a small child. Just through the pumping music, I could hear the familiar chuckle from the boy I was laying on, he then whispered some other lyrics in my ear, right before I passed out. The sound of his voice drifting into my ear was what I blacked out to.

"*Can we fast forward to go down on me?*"

# Chapter 29

A soft purring under me, and a warm hand intertwining my fingers with their own, is what I woke up to. I unstuck my eyelids from each other and peeked at where I was. I saw Romeo, driving with a soft smile on his face. When I looked down, I saw his hand clasping onto mine, casually laying on his thigh. I opened my eyes fully and pulled my hand away as he reluctantly let go. I coughed some and rubbed my sore eyes, pulling my hair out from under me and sat the enormous clump in my lap. I put some strands behind my ears and yawned. "Ugh, I have such a horrible headache." I sat my back against the seat and sighed, "I wasn't dreaming and we really did go to an awesome party right?"

He chuckled and watched me out of the corner of his eye, with what seemed like...a blush on his face? What? "Yes, Scarlett, we did go to a party." I groaned in pain at the hammer inside my head, pounding away.

"I- I remember going to get a drink, tasting something weird, then everything after that I completely- it's all nothing to me, I don't remember a clue of it." His smile dropped almost immediately and he slammed his foot on the break, the gravel from the vacant road we were riding on flew everywhere. His voice was so low it kind of scared me.

"You *what*?" I started at him and his jet black hair in fear from his response to my sudden amnesia.

"I said, I don't remember." His eyes seemed glossy and he faced the road again, slamming his foot on the acceleration. He threw his head back and laughed almost insane sounding. His black eyes blazed as his smile seemed particularly evil.

"Oh yes! I almost forgot!" He took a sharp turn, smacking his hands on the wheel several times, creating the car to obnoxiously beep over and over. His voice lowered and his glossy eyes became shinier as his jaw clenched, unclenched then he smiled again, almost as if he had lost his damn mind. "The drugs wear off later!" I almost choked on my own spit as my glasses fell down the bridge of my nose.

"*What*?!" I smacked his arm as hard as I could, and immediately clutched it, pain searing through my whole arm from my elbow stretching to my finger tips. "What the fuck do you mean *drugs*- I *know* I didn't take any fucking *drugs*!" he laughed again and smacked the wheel one more time.

"Oh- but you did, Scarlett!" He scratched his forehead, "Some were in that drink and more was in that brownie you ate. Don't be surprised if your purging later!" He laughed one more time and braked really hard. "Have fun pondering on how our night went earlier, Scarlett!" He turned me to hold eye contact, his eyes angry and his mouth smiling. "Were here." I nodded, my jaw clenched, still angry at him. Almost as if in a demanding tone he spoke to me again, finalizing everything. "*Goodbye*." He eyed something near my legs and I looked down to see my clothes and belongings. He opened the doors and I got out as quickly slamming the door shut as hard as I could. He zoomed off in the distance and I turned around, my ears tearing up, to find Sarah, Ivy, and Bambi, mouths hanging open.

Almost as if it was planned they all said in unison-

"Holy,"

"Fucking,"

"Shit."

I sped into the house and slammed my butt down on the couch, almost immediately they all ran to me and shot me questions.

"What happened?!" Bambi asked.

"What are you wearing?!" Ivy shot.

"Are you okay?!" Sarah demanded

"What did he do to you?!" Bambi questioned.

"I'm gonna fucking kill him!" Ivy exclaimed.

"*Guys! Shut the fuck up!*" I yelled over all of their questions.

"He took me to a picnic, we had a juice fight, we painted a mural, we partied, I accidentally took some drugs, I don't remember the rest of the night and when I told Romeo I didn't he practically went ballistic on me- I don't know what I did or what I've done, I don't know what the fuck is going on and my brain can't even process what I did after I took that drink and that brownie all I know is what I did effected Romeo, I am wearing his shirt and a bikini under this, I am okay, he didn't do anything to me- I don't think and don't fucking kill him yet because I need answers first!" I pressed my hands to my temples and shut my eyes as they sighed in response to my persisted, rushed babbling.

"Tell us about the whole night." Ivy and Sarah pressed. Bambi just shook her head in a non-approving manner.

"I knew from the start that he would be trouble. Trouble and an ass."

"Okay, so we ate sandwiches and he played his guitar, then we had a juice fight-"

"What is a juice fight?" Sarah interrupted.

"We had tons of cups of juice and we threw it at each other, therefore causing a juice fight. Anyways, we did that then we- oh wait." I looked all through the pile of stuff in my hands and pulled out a mangled photo. I smoothed out the wrinkles and handed it to them with an unamused look on my face. "He wrote the caption."

They all smirked but when they saw the picture, their mouths dropped. "You guys look like a couple, why is he kissing you?" I rolled my eyes and snatched it back.

"At the last minute, he kissed my cheek." They chewed on their lips and I continued. "Anyways we had the juice fight, and then on that white wall you saw in the background, we used that to make a mural. Then he got a call from his friend Louche, about a party- which I told Bambi about," Bambi shook her head in annoyance. "Anyways, it was the best party I have ever been too by the way. You should of seen it. But of course there were a lot of drugs which I tried to prevent myself from, so I took a drink of something fruity with this nasty after taste, then ate a brownie- which according to Romeo, both had drugs in them, and..." I shut my eyes again trying to remember- it was slowly coming back in little bits.

93

"*And?*" Ivy stabbed at me with.

"And...I remember dancing with him again then feeling nauseous...then I fell because my whole body felt all ticklish, and I was giggling the whole time. And..." The next part of the memory fuzzed into view and I felt my eyes go wide. The kiss, the feeling of kissing him, everything came back right there at that moment. "And uh..." I glanced at the girls and bit my lip and shook my head, looking to the right. "And I guess I fell asleep while he was carrying me back to the car." Bambi's eyes blazed with anger and she laughed without humor.

"You liar! Your looking to the bottom right! Your lying!" I bit my lip harder.

"I swear! That's it!" I stood up along with Bambi and Sarah stood up beside me.

"Bambi's right, you're lying- I know when you're lying by your face, Scarlett." She said softly putting a hand on my shoulder. "You can tell us, we won't judge you. That includes Bambi, right Bambi?" Sarah spot-lighted Bambi and Bambi nodded sullenly. "Yes."

I did a one-over of all of them, "Do you guys really want to know, now that I remember?" They all nodded, and Ivy nodded with excitement. I sighed in defeat, "I kissed him. No- more like I attacked him- more like I *killed his lips with my tongue.*" Ivy made a grossed out face.

"Way to be vivid, Scar-Scar."

I glared at her, "I didn't exactly know what I was doing at the time. All I remember was that I was really into it, he was really into it- and I felt something weird. Like...*need.*"

"Didn't I tell you that you would fall for him? I did, remember?!" Bambi shot at me still cautious of the situation.

"Can we please just forget about this? I just had a horrible-slash-amazing time, and I kinda want to forget about it okay?" I sat back down and rubbed my eyes.

"Well I think I can change that." A deep, flirtatious, male voice came from the back of the room. I jumped and I could hear everyone stop breathing, including me.

A nice, lean, tan young man in a muscle shirt and cut off shorts leaned against the door frame of what seemed like a slide glass door, which I, for the first time, noticed.

"Hidalgo, what are you doing here?" He chuckled and uncrossed his arms. "May I come in, Bambi?" She nodded and smiled in response to seeing him instead of Romeo.

"Can I get you anything Hidalgo? A drink or food?" He smiled and shuffled his way inside, answering with a small shake of his head and a smug smile across his face.

"So, you *attacked* a boy's lips with your *tongue?*" He sat down in a recliner chair and shook his head, "Sounds like you got hot and heavy with one of the collage boys, Scarlett. Did you have fun tonight or what?" He chuckled and nodded at Ivy. "Your right, very vivid response."

I felt myself rip a few strands of hair out of my head. "When exactly did you start listening to the conversation?" He smiled with a cute kind of evil in it.

94

"Walked in right when you got to the dirty details. Like I said, fun night or what?" I flicked the strands to the side and buried my face in my hands.

"Oh my god." I managed to muffle out from the warmness of my flesh.

"So who's the lucky guy, Scarlett?" He chuckled and I glared at him through my hands.

"I am anything but lucky feeling, right now."

"Aw, no score? No home-run with this one?" I removed my hands so he can see my glare.

"Shut up, I am sure Romeo had a great time though." I sighed and sat back on the couch, then threw a pillow over my head.

"You kissed Romeo?" I could feel all the teasing and playfulness in his voice gone. I didn't want to look at him- I was too ashamed of the look he would probably give me.

"Yes."

"Do you like him?"

"No!" But I knew I answered too quick so that he wouldn't believe me. I removed the pillow from my face and pushed up my glasses that were falling off. "No." I said again, more calmly.

"That's fine, whatever you do with other people is your business." He clenched his jaw though, telling me he still disapproved.

"Okay what is up with you and Romeo? Do you guys have some kind of beef or something?" Ivy interjected, almost making me jump because I completely forgot that she was there.

"Me and Romeo have...our differences." He put his hands together in his lap, curling his lip and watched the floor.

"What happened, you can tell me." I put my hand on his arm and felt as his arm pulsated from the tensing up he was doing.

"He tries to get chummy with my sister, and I wouldn't say I enjoy watching him feel her up constantly." I felt his arm slowly unclench from my touch.

"Who is your sister?" I thought for a minute but then put it together. "Wait a minute its-"

He looked up from the floor at me and nodded. "Nina."

"But I thought it's just dancing?" He nodded and turned back to watching the floor.

"I have no issue with them dancing, but when it comes to after dancing, her always sneaking out to see him in the middle of the night- leaving her chores to me in the mornings because she's not back in time, upsetting our mother, Manuela, having me take the blame for her because I am supposed to watch after her? No, I don't accept that- I have no respect for him. Even little Alejandro misses her to death. He's one of my little brothers- as well as Aleksandr, an orphan we took in on the streets of Cuba back when he was just a *niño pequeño*. Then we have little Maria, Adalia, Clemente, Benita, Esteban, and Esme." I felt my eyes go wide.

"How many siblings is that?!"

"Including me, my mother has had nine children."

"Holy shit, can you say all their names for me again?!"

"Hidalgo, Alejandro, Aleksandr, Maria, Clemente, Benita, Esteban, and Esme."

"Whoa!" Sarah, Ivy, and Bambi said at the same time- wicked smiles across their faces.

"Is it just with one dad? What's his name?" Bambi asked.

"My father was a great man, his name was Javier. But hes gone into the heavens right now." He gave me a soft smile and I felt my heart break. "I know god sees him as a great man."

"I am sure he was an amazing human being." I said softly and he smiled to himself.

"He is the one that actually taught me to dance. His name is actually Javier Jr. because my grandfather Javier Senior thought that he should live on his culture and have a true Cuban heart. My whole family timeline traces back to the revolution of Castro. It is all very amazing. But I think we got way off topic here." He narrowed his eyes at the ground and clenched his fists. "Excuse my language around you, because you are a lady, but Romeo is a jackass and a man-whore. If I could I would kill him right now for what he does, but I don't want to upset Nina."

"I don't blame you, and I only kissed him because I was intoxicated with drugs- I didn't know what I was doing." His eyes flashed with panic.

"You take drugs?!" His brown eyes widened and he ran a hand through his hair.

"No! It was an accident- the thing I ate and drank was spiked!" He let out a breath and smiled a little.

"You scared me there. But I want to kind of say thank you."

"Why?" I stroked my long black hair, and raised my eyebrows.

"Because Nina hasn't really hung out with him, or snuck out with him ever since he's been interested in you. He keeps rejecting her and she's kind of upset." He bit his lip, I wasn't sure if it was in guilt or just a habit.

"Should I be saying 'your welcome' or should I be flattered by this?" I got up from the couch and stormed into the hallway until he grabbed my arm and spun me around.

"Scarlett I am saying thank you because your relieving the things that cause my life a living hell." I was aware that music was playing in the background and that Bambi never shut it off. "Your the someone that fixes my everything." He slid a little bit closer to me on the carpet and I couldn't catch my breath. I was still very, very angry at him. "Scarlett, you're the only one I have ever danced with in seven years."

Instead of looking down at the ground, avoiding his eyes, I gazed up at him. "You picked me." I said softly, barely a whisper. He nodded and dragged his hand down my forearm until he intertwined his fingers with mine.

"I sit at the dancing practices with the others and don't dance. I don't speak and just watch my sister. When I first saw you it was like your eyes were glowing with a fire I have never seen in anyone, the fire of a dancer. I knew right then and there that I wanted it, wanted *you* to be with me. To dance with me. Now I think that I have done my part very well to try to get you to like me as much as I like you, because Scarlett- you're the one, the only one that I ever want to dance with. *All* that I am asking is if you are willing to return the favor?"

I felt the wind escape my lungs, I heard my heard pounding in my ears and the background music of 'Called Out in The Dark' by Snow Patrol in the distance, I could feel his heartbeat in his pulse in his wrist that my wrist was touching, I could smell strawberries and cinnamon soap, and the only thing I saw before me were eyes. Big, beautiful, chocolate brown eyes.

"Hidalgo, I..." I looked from his eyes from his lips. "I..."

"Kiss me, then tell me what you think then." He said softly, a small smile touching his lips.

I nodded, my face scrunching up in the pain of the intense moment, in response to our body heat, our energy, touching. I took a step closer and he grabbed my forearms. I stood there; looking at his chest then closed my eyes. I just listened to our breathing for a couple dozen seconds. "Do you think that this is the right thing?" He slowly pulled my hand and put it up to his heart, which was speeding and probably ricocheting off the walls of the inside of his chest. He then put his hand on my heart, which he could probably feel the exact same.

"Tell me...what do you think?" I clenched my eyes shut and put my free arm around his waist, but kept my hand on his heart, which he didn't move, his hand above my heart and did the exact same too. I pushed myself up a little on the tips of my toes, and felt our noses brush.

"I have been thinking about this for too long." He whispered and I smiled a little then he slowly kissed my top lip. My bottom one kissed his and when we pulled away, he opened his eyes- afraid of what my reaction was going to be. When I opened my eyes, I stared at him for a couple seconds, and then trusted my heart to pull the strings that moved my body.

I felt myself go numb, but I thought I smiled. His response was hugging me and saying two words.

"Thank you."

# Chapter 30

Shakira. That was the only thing we listened to a little after that.

Not only because Bambi liked her, but because that was the only Cuban or Latin music she could think of from the top of her head.

"Move like- yes, like that. See you got it!" He had Ivy's hands in his own and they both did a little shake-and-shuffle thing with their hips. She was laughing like crazy and he smiled brightly. She wrapped her leg around his and he dipped her. She giggled and looked at me upside down.

"Scarlett, you have great taste in guys." I smiled and laughed, pulling my hair back and doing a ponytail by tying it in a knot by itself. Hidalgo chuckled and pulled her back up and she jumped up and down then hugged him in a friendly way. "Oh my god, that was so much fun!"

I laughed and Hidalgo held out a hand for me to stand up with him. "I think we need to show these girls what I've taught you. Shall we?" I laughed and nodded.

"We shall!" The girls laughed and cheered, all of them sitting in a row on the couch. The computer flipped to the next track. One of the more played, famous ones came on called 'Hips Don't Lie'.

When he yanked me close they all screamed louder. He gave me a mischievous smile and I spun out from his arms and back in, to a tight curl. I shook my hips back and forth while taking a couple steps forward and a couple steps back in unison with him. We swung our arms and out of nowhere he took my hand and spun me in a ballerina circle. I shimmied and laughed as he slid his hands down and crouched his hands down. The girls whistled and cheered, and he grabbed a clump of my dress, that I put on in place of the t-shirt. He sprung up and grabbed my hand and spun me out again, flinging my dress in the air so it would flit out as I swept across the room. I walked towards him and put a hand on his chest pushing him back against the wall, where he ducked out from under me and turned so that I turned to be against the wall. He grabbed my waist and my hand and pulled me out in a couple steps backward. We both shook and shimmied at each other. I got close to him and he grabbed my waist and I hung back, dipping myself as he swung my torso near the ground, my hair sweeping across the floor. He pulled me back up and I put my leg around his and he pulled up on my arms swinging my body back and forth on his sides. I laughed and backed up from him, shaking out my hair, and Ivy, Sarah, and Bambi erupted in, "Whoop!" and "Go Scarlett!". I felt on fire, and I liked that. This feeling of being rejuvenated. I spun towards him and he rapped his arm around me and kissed me lightly just before the song ended. I smiled brightly and pulled away from him, us both bowing.

"You guys are great!" Sarah said lightly, clapping softly. "That is so cool that you guys can do that." I glanced at Romeo who was still smiling at watching me, I smiled in response to our hands that were still holding together. A knock on the door snapped us out of it.

"I'll get it." Ivy said winking at the two of us. We both blushed and I bumped into him. Ivy opened the front door, which I couldn't see who was behind it. Her eyes turned into daggers and she slammed the door on whoever it was' face. They pounded on the door and yelled from the other side.

"Common, Scarlett, let me in!" They whined, pounding harder.

"Who the hell is that?!" Bambi asked, all frightened. I pushed past her, completely forgetting about Hidalgo and looked through the peep hole. He pounded some more and I watched as his magnified head set itself on the door, finally quitting.

"I got this." I said in a low voice and opened the door and slammed my body into his so that he would back off the house. I shut the door behind me and put a hand on his chest, shoving him farther and farther away. He back stepped all the way until we were about a good half block away from the house. "Do you want to die today? Because I can do that!" I raised my fist at him as a threat and he ran backwards a little bit, trying to get some space but I just kept following every step he made with a step of my own, with my fist raised.

"Scarlett- stoppit! Now!" He yelled at me but that just made me madder.

"Oh, don't try your high and mighty act with me, Shane, you know I am not ready for your bullshit!" He put his hands up in surrender and as a sign that he meant no harm. "Don't even try to fuck with me right now, you're the last person I ever want to see." He took a brave step forward and I moved my fist higher, cautioning him. He put his hands down and grabbed my fist with his tattooed hand and shoved it to my side.

"And don't *your* high and mighty act, Scarlett, we both know that you're as fragile as a flower when it comes to your feelings and your fighting." He furrowed his eyebrows and three little lines appeared between them. I shook my head and laughed dryly.

"Yeah, you should know right? Like that one time you slapped the shit out of me when you were drunk?" He flinched but he recovered quickly as usual, running a hand through his freshly cut and trim black hair.

"I was drunk, not like that's any excuse, but still- it was one time. I don't know what you're so bitchy about, about that." He shrugged and put his thumbs in his belt rings on his black pants, the sound of the leather rubbing together on his arms from his jacket. His short foe-hawk shiny in the moonlight and a little gold glare from the porch light at Bambi's house far away. I remember when I liked the *old* Shane. When he was all sweater-vests and pocket protectors. How he would make jokes about how we always had a certain sort of chemistry all along, explaining how we were both just molecules and that we would always move on, whether it was always and forever together or something happened. I think the something happened, big time.

"I had a bruised face for two weeks- so yes, I will bitch over it. I could fucking get you arrested for that, and I probably will." He put his hand on my shoulder which I smacked away almost instantly with the best force that I had in my hand.

"You don't want to do that, Scarlett. That's a lot of drama we don't need." He rubbed his eyes and pinched the bridge of his nose, with a hand on his hip.

"*This* is a lot of drama we don't need." He sighed in a sort of 'here we go again' type of way. I pointed between me and him. "Leave, and never come back. Or I *will* bring authorities into this, and I have plenty to tell them."

"Whatever, came here to ask for you back but you lost your chance. Bye."

"If you even thought I would say yes, your more of an idiot than I gave you credit for. Goodbye." He started to turn around but I nodded to myself, "Wait."

He turned back around with a smug grin on his face, I walked up to him and slapped him as hard as I could in the face. "Wipe that grin off your face before you go."

I then spun around and stalked back to the house, clenching my jaw. I walked through the door and they all were sitting on the couches and chair staring into space. When they heard me open the door they all stood up and stood there awkwardly.

"So...who was that?" Sarah said, but the look on her face told me that she already knew.

"No one worth caring about, that's for sure." they all nodded to themselves and I walked over and sat my Hidalgo.

"Should I be worried, *chica*?"

"No its fine." I nodded and smiled. Bambi sighed and stood up smiling down at Hidalgo apologetically.

"I am sorry, but we have some stuff that we need to do for the rest of the night, but it was so amazing having you over, come anytime." Bambi winked at the both of us and she smiled. The girls smiled too, and I hugged Hidalgo.

"Bye."

"Bye." He had a blush creep across his face before he left with shutting the door lightly.

Bambi clapped her hands together, "So...are any of you into tattoos?"

# Chapter 31

"This is stupid."

"I'm afraid of needles!"

"Why, Bambi? Why?!"

"Everyone just shut the fuck up. You will see." We all stopped whining and bounced on her bed. Bambi was rummaging through her closet and I watched as many pink and many sparkly things were showing.

I realized some things about Bambi, assumptions that were way off. One, Bambi was really nice, but she also knew how to be a bitch with people who crossed her, she wasn't all tears and ice cream when it came to the problems she had. Two, she wasn't all innocent as she seemed to be, for crying out loud- she was talking about tattoos right now. I don't even like tattoos anyways, I thought they would look trashy on me if I got one. Three, she acted a lot younger than she seemed to be. She made a lot of kiddish decisions, yet she knew the right thing to do. Maybe it was right being a kid more than an adult sometimes. Last but not least, Bambi had more clothes than I could have seen in a department store stuffed in her closet than I have seen ever fit in any ones home, let alone a *closet* before.

"Sizes, cough them up." I didn't bother looking at my tag, I already fit in Bambi's clothing, even if my upper chest did spill out a little more.

"You already know I fit into your clothes." I lay down on her bed, but clenched my legs together so that no one would see my crotch. Ivy laughed and lay down next to me.

"Yeah, you fit in her clothes but your boobs don't." Bambi giggled and moved some more hangers over, creating an uncomfortable screeching noise.

"Oh look, my costume from... three Halloweens ago?" She pulled out an orange and black witch costume and a little contacts case. She opened them up to show us some cool orange contact lenses. Sarah grabbed them and picked one up at the tip of her finger to look at them.

"That is so neat." Ivy sat back up.

"I am a size three." Sarah nodded and gave the contact lenses back.

"Me too." Bambi flipped her orange-blond hair out of the way and smiled, her freckles stretching just a little bit across her cheek bones.

"Great. Put this stuff on," She rummaged a little then pulled out a dress with a black torso, a buckle on the middle belt that hung a little low and a floral skirt attached to it. She chucked it at Sarah and pointed to the bathroom for her to change.

"Ivy, you seem like a complicated creature for me to style." Ivy sat up and glared at her.

"Wow, thanks Bambi for the kind words." Bambi rolled her eyes.

"I didn't mean it in a bad way, cranky pants. Here." She pulled out a short, strapless, camouflage dress and a matching jacket. "Report to the bathroom, and here," She threw a make up bag at her as well and several hair appliances. "You and Sarah get ready in there, and I am going to mess with the beast in here." Bambi shuffled over to me and grabbed a clump of my hair and shook it in Ivy's face. "This might take awhile." I gasped.

"Hey!"

"Well its true!" Bambi let go of my hair and shooed Ivy out of the bedroom. Once the door clicked shut Bambi turned around and sighed. "So. Much. Work." She came over and took my tied ponytail out of its knot and started twisting it. Once it was coiled she wrapped it around my head and took several giant clips to hold it in place. She ripped a bunch of clothes off hangers and threw them all over her room. "Are you a girly girl?" I shook my head.

"Well kind of, I don't really have a preference. I dress the way I feel I guess." She smiled and sat back against her closet door.

"So if I made you all girly you wouldn't care?" I shook my head and she nodded, still smiling. She plunged back into her closet and laughed. "Yes! I found the perfect thing!" She pulled out a short, *really short*, pink sequin dress.

"I will freeze to death!" She shook her head and grabbed my arm gesturing for me to get up, I stood and she held it up on me.

"Beauty is pain, Scarlett, beauty is pain..." She looked at me holding the dress up to myself for her at other angles and nodded to herself grabbing the dress and putting it on the bed. "Strip." I peeled off the other dress and pulled the pink on over my head. I slipped my bra off from under it and adjusted my body inside the tight fabric. "You look great!" I smiled and hugged my arms, already cold.

"Now gimme your head." She unclasped all the clips on my head and let my hair fall to my thigh. She spun me around. "Actually all you really need is a run through your hair with my straightener and you should be fine." She plugged in a big lug of a straightener and let it heat up. She sprayed heat protecting spray into my hair and I brushed through it. She then went to work on my head. Once she was finished which seemed like an hour and a half later, she yelled at the door. "Hey! We're still going, are you guys done?"

"No!" She nodded and pulled a bunch of fake pink, sparkly flowers out from a box in the back of her closet and started snipping off the stems. She pinned them all with bobby pins and set them on the bed while she pulled the outside layer of my hair up and put hairspray underneath. She sprayed the back some more then pulled the front of my hair back and started braiding it, pinning the braid to the back of my head with the flowers. She stepped back to look at her work.

"Okay... it's perfect. Don't move." She pulled out a makeup box and pulled out a greenish-yellow eye shadow and started lightly applying it on my eyes. She put winged tips on my eyelids and then applied some mascara on my eyelashes. She put some powder all over my face, concealer, then took a little brush from her set and dipped it in some pink goop. She put it on carefully and then mixed in a clear lip gloss coat on top.

She handed me some pink heels and I slipped them on. I stood up and she smiled at her work.

"You look phenomenal." I smiled and she put her hand over her mouth smiling too.

"We're finished!" Sarah yelled from the bathroom. I heard the bathroom door open and I looked at myself in her vanity mirror. I put my hands on my cheeks in awe.

"Oh my god, I look great." Bambi giggled and she opened the door. I heard Ivy and Sarah clomp through and I slowly turned around. They put their hands on their mouths and they both gasped, wide eyed.

"Oh my god, Scarlett!" Ivy walked over and I spun around for them, she glanced at my huge braid in the back laying on my hair and her smile was bigger than ever.

"You look fantastic!" Sarah came over too and lightly hugged me, "I have to be careful, and I don't wanna mess up your hair." She chuckled and smiled brightly as well, scooting closer to Ivy.

"Bambi- what are you going to wear?" Bambi put her hands on her hips and blew the bangs out of her face.

"Well... you guys wanna help me have a makeover? I do this every year or so. Drastically change my look. Last year I was a nerd, I lost my contacts and bought nerdy glasses instead and wore suspenders and stuff. I am thinking of going scene this year." She moved her hair on her neck to her shoulder and stood there, thinking back to memories while we all stared at her.

"Are you serious? You have only been like this for a year?" Sarah piped up, Bambi laid down on the bed, nodding. "So what's the real you?" Bambi sighed in frustration.

"That's just it. I don't really know who I am, all I know is that if I don't change myself all the time- I will lose myself, and no one wants that." Sarah sat down next to her and patted her stomach.

"Don't worry. You will some day." Bambi nodded in agreement then sat up.

"Okay, well I am going to get the hair dye. Be right back. Oh and Scarlett, you can't help." I moved a strand out from the front of my eye and frowned at her, slapping my hands on my calves.

"Why not me?!" She smiled at me with sympathy, trying to look sweet.

"Because I spent too long on making you look like *that*. I am not even risking you ruining any of it." She waggled her hands in front of my face and I swatted them away, crossing my arms, pouting. They all headed out to the bathroom and I took a seat in the chair by her vanity and gazed at myself in her mirror, running the strand of hair hanging in my face over and over inside my two fingers. I waited and examined her makeup and hair stuff on the desk. She had a lot of pretty sounding brands that I was aware of and some of them I knew nothing about. She had made up from New York and a blue straightener from Australia. Her barrettes came from Brazil and her earrings were bought and sent overseas from Russia. Everything sitting in front of my eyes were either sparkly, colorful, expensive or all of the above. About fifteen minutes later, Ivy yelled from the

103

other room that her hair was done, and I heard a hairdryer shut off. Bambi sauntered in the room and flipped her hair, which by the way was bright and shiny orange. I walked over to her and ran my fingers through it like people have been doing to my hair the past couple days.

"It looks good Bambi." I smiled lightly at her and she giggled slightly. Ivy and Sarah shuffled in as well and smiled at they work. I glanced down to see their Orange-brown dyed hands and frowned. "You guys are going to see some good hard soap to wash that off..." They peered down at their hands too.

"Aw!" they both whined and ran back into the bathroom, soon the sound of a faucet tinkling into a sink made its way into the bedroom and I listened as they groaned while they scrubbed their hands. The doorbell rang and a couple raps on the door sounded and Bambi opened the door, greeting someone. I waited patiently in the bedroom but eavesdropped on their conversation.

"Hey, Drake, what's up?" I heard Bambi say in a friendly tone.

"Oh, nothing really, just got some of your mail in my box again, here." There was a pause. "Nice hair by the way, I really like it." I could hear the smile in his voice.

"Oh thanks. Just dyed it five minutes ago." She followed that by a nervous giggle.

"Oh okay, well I will see you later. Have a fun night, Bambi. Bye."

Bambi did the nervous laugh again. "Yeah no problem, thanks, bye." Then I heard the shut of the front door. I could her feet squeaking against the wood floor in the hall way.

"Scarlett! You got something in *my* mailbox!" She quickly squeaked her way into the bedroom and handed me a pressed, designed envelope that had my name printed on it in swirly print. I grabbed a sharp nail file from her desk and tried but failed to carefully rip the top. I took out a periwinkle, nice, floral decorated paper and unfolded the hard creased remains, reading out loud what the lovely print on the inside said.

"Scarlett Tod, you are cordially invited to a late dinner at the home of Meredith Monroe and her son on the twenty-third of March at nine PM. We expect your presence, please come." I glanced at the clock and read the time. It was eight thirty-seven at night.

"Oh god, what is the date?" Bambi shook her head and grabbed a cell phone off her bedside table and flipped it open.

"It's the twenty-third!" I stood up abruptly and Ivy and Sarah ran in the bedroom.

"What's wrong?" They both said at the same time.

"But what about our fun tonight?" Bambi whined in defeat. I shook my head and glanced at the invitation again for a sign of hope.

"Ah! See here? I can take as many people as I want as long as it goes up to five at the highest. You all can come with me to the rich lady's house!" Ivy shook out her hands, arching her back so none got on her dress.

"Sounds fine with me, and Bambi we can do all that stuff afterwards. It's okay, really." Bambi bit her lip.

104

"Well I really wanted to put an impression on you guys and have fun because you guys seemed to hate me the last time we saw each other. That's all I wanted." Bambi lowered her head down so that she was looking at her bare feet in sadness. I patted her back and gestured between me and the other girls.

"She has been trying really hard to make you guys like her. She was stressing big time when I told her you guys were coming over." Ivy scrunched up her nose in guilt and Sarah pouted, tapping Bambi on the shoulder.

"You see, it wasn't that we didn't like you- you just caught us in a really horrible time is all. It isn't the most pleasant first impression to put on someone when your yelling at them because your best friend is in the hospital."

"Yeah," Ivy agreed and smiled slightly. "We are the wrong people you need to worry about impressions anyways." Bambi laughed in all her sweetness and bit her lip.

"So we're good?" They all nodded, Ivy clearly amused.

"Psst, yes!" I smiled and grabbed some pink knee high boots and zipped them on instead.

"I need to make sure that I don't trip on my way to running to the car." I laughed and waved them, jogging out the door- my boobs holding me back, making me slower as I tried to run. "Come on guys!" we all ran out the door, and I hopped in the passenger seat of Bambi's Bug and the girls piled in the back then Bambi jumped in, I noticed in a completely different outfit. "H-how did you do that?!" Bambi shook her head.

"Drive now, questions later. Lemme see that invitation." I handed it to her with my cold hands and she flipped the heat on, taking it out of parking and whipped the car out, driving with her elbows on the wheel while she read something off the little piece of paper. She threw it at me, and floored the car. She was driving almost as erratic as Romeo was earlier and I tried to lean back in my seat but she snapped at me. "The flowers, Scarlett, the *flowers*." I leaned forward and put my elbows on my knees, trying not to smack my face on her glove box every time she lurched forward or screeched to a stop. She slowed down and pulled in front a huge mansion gate.

# Chapter 32

Some guards suspiciously shone their flashlights in our faces.

"What is your business here?" A tall, dark haired, handsome one asked Bambi, and I piped up.

"My name is Scarlett Tod, and these are the guests that I invited along. I was sent this invitation to come to dinner with a Meredith Monroe?" I handed the guard on my side of the car my little invite in its envelope. He looked over it for a minute then nodded to the other guard.

"She can go in." The other one nodded in response and called in a number inside a wake-talkie. Then the gate opened and she handed the keys to a valet. Scarlett led the others to the front door, to where the door was opened for them by a butler.

"Scarlett, we've been expecting you." I glanced back at the others and they grinned at me with amusement as we all walked through the door. The mansion was incredible with a triple staircase and big, bright chandelier. The woman from the night of the cotillion, slowly made her way down the middle staircase. She glanced down at her watch, an extravagant smile on her face, and clicked her way off the last two steps of the staircase and spread her arms in a greeting manor.

"Ah, Scarlett, you came- and right on the dot of nine too. Welcome, welcome! And who are these lovely ladies of yours?" She smiled, in a way that couldn't be described as anything other than *plastic*. She made her way towards me, dismissively looking at them and started to stare at my hair. Before they got their names out she started shooting more questions my way. "Are you wearing a wig?" I heard a little gasp of hurt come from Bambi from behind me, from Meredith's comment about her work on my hair.

"No, I am not. This is my..." It was hard to get the words out considering they meant more things than one, "Natural hair." I managed to choke out of my throat. It wasn't the truth but it wasn't a lie. I pointed at them as I named them off, turning my back on her. "This is Sarah, Ivy, and lastly Bambi, by the way, Meredith." She plastered on a smile again.

"Oh, well hello, hello! Let's get on to the late dinner." She trailed on to a grand dining room in the next room and we followed, taking seats as the butler pushed them in for all of us.

"So, I have to tell you. I have no clue why you invited me to your house, Ms. Monroe." She nodded and set her chin on her delicately manicured hands.

"Yes, yes." She said barely above a whisper, her voice almost chiming as beautifully as the classical music playing the background. She was in a dinner dress and her hair was perfectly falling into place as if she woke up every morning and never had to do a thing to it. I heard little tinkling of the fountain in her lawn outside the window, and the lights above my head seemed as if the starlight put power into them. I felt...small in her presence for some reason. I always thought that it was stereotypical that rich people repeat things to sound more sophisticated. "Well I wasn't about to let you slip right out of my fingers." She continued as the food was set on our table. She started to grab thing with engraved ladles and we followed suit. "I still have the offer for the acting audition on the table and I still am interested in letting you in on this career. But you never called back so I thought I better have the upper hand on getting a hold of you instead." I nodded remembering back to the night where she gave me her card right after I...

"Actually, I have had tragic events happen and I am, emotionally, in no place to initiate anything." She nodded. And I put some vegetables on my plate along with a chicken breast while someone poured wine in my glass and the others too.

"Loss of a loved one?" I gulped down my tears, and I felt my ears grow hot talking about it.

"My mother died." She nodded again, not fazed by the topic.

"The woman that you were angry at that night?" I nodded and tried hard to swallow my dry food with a dry throat. Once I barely got it down, I took a sip of my hard red wine to wash it down, trying really hard not to cringe at the horrible tasting drink.

"Do you like the red wine? Malbec." I nodded and planted my best fake smile as well.

"Oh it's just amazing and great." She nodded, seeming to buy it. She blew off the whole thing about my mom and kept going on about the job.

"So do you think you would still be interested?" I shook my head, spearing a broccoli with my silver fork.

"I am sorry to say that I am not comfortable with being called for a job for acting on my looks one bad night. I also have never acted in my life." I thought to myself that that was a lie though. I acted for many years to my mother that everything was fine with me while behind closed doors, I was being molested by my dad. I was a terrible liar to Meredith this moment. I was the best actress I knew- but not in that kind of way.

"Well, fine then. But you will come back, the offer always stands. You already have my card. I know I am forgetting something..." She glanced around the table and snapped her fingers in a way that I thought would pop off one of her fake nails, like mine always did when I bought them from the dollar store.

"That son of mine. He skipped a guest dinner again. Charlie- go fetch my son for dinner, tell him to meet me in the living room and that I am not waiting up for him." One of the butlers nodded to her and swiftly made his way into the living room and disappeared around the corner. She excused herself and did the same, leaving us girls sitting there. We started whispering.

"I wonder if her son is hot- do you Sarah?" Sarah shook her head.

"Oh I forgot you have a man of your own now, *Sarah*." Sarah started to get panicked on us.

"What? No!" I gave her a look.

"Okay answer these questions as fast as you can, without even thinking okay?" She nodded and sat back in her chair.

"Favorite color?"

"Blue."

"Favorite show?"

"Television is stupid."

"Siblings?"

"One."

"Boyfriend?"

"Vladimir." I smiled evilly in victory and Sarah put a hand over her mouth and shook her head frantically. "N-no wait. I didn't mean like a *boyfriend* I meant like a boy who is a-"

"I want to meet him!" Bambi giggled and Ivy high-fived her lightly.

"We both do!" I smiled at Bambi and Ivy's tag teaming. Bambi pulled a cell phone out of her pocket and handed it to Sarah for the night.

"He is going to pick you up afterwards." She shook her head and tossed it back to Bambi.

"No." All of our mouths hung open and we all whispered-yelled to her at the same time.

"You are!"

"No!" Sarah whined tapping her flats over and over on the ground like a five year old.

"We'll talk about this later." I said and Ivy shushed us all.

"I think I hear footsteps!" Bambi and Ivy checked each other for any flaws in their appearance, and me and Sarah watched them in embarrassment. They were so cute though, worrying about guys like they were in middle school. I heard a sigh coming from some else and I heard Meredith and her son bickering back and forth. I couldn't quite make out what they were saying from the other room but the bickering came to a stop and I could hear the clicking of Meredith's heels as she made her way closer. She started speaking to us from the other room.

"Girls, this is my son-" She soon came into the room with a very familiar boy trailing behind her. "Romeo." We all gasped and I clenched my jaw as a very trim, neat, clean, Romeo made its way into the dining room. When he heard a gasp he looked up from watching his feet, took one look at me, then walked over quickly grabbing my arm, pulling me out of my seat and pushing past his mother, dragging me along.

"We need to talk." I tried to get out of his grasp but he wouldn't let me go. Dumbfounded his mom yelled from behind us.

"You guys know each other?!"

"Romeo, let me go, now!" He just clenched his jaw and pulled me along harder, his force very strong. He dragged me up the stairs and down some long halls, he shoved me into a gargantuan room and the first thing that I noticed was our mural, front and center, right there on the biggest wall I have ever seen. It looked like it belonged in a cathedral. The next thing that caught my eye was a big black bed, pressed against the wall in front of me, then the black velvet and silk sheets that lay lazily around the perimeter of the bed. I glanced on the right of the room and saw a full twenty set of guitars, a growing collection with many paintings hung above them. Replicas of famous paintings hung all over the white wall that I was looking at. *Starry Night, The Tenth Wave, La Promenade, Misty Mood* and *Alley By The Lake* were some of the featured ones, from artists like Vincent Van Gogh, Ivan Konstantinovich Aivazovsky, Claude Monet, and Leonid Afremov. They all were beautiful and matched Romeo's personality much. I realized just then that I was in Romeo's bedroom.

His bedroom looked more like it should be a living room instead of the one downstairs and the one downstairs shouldn't even be his bedroom. My bedroom could take up about a ninth of his bedroom. "The drugs apparently didn't wear off yet because you're sitting in my house, in my chairs, talking to *my* mother." I felt my eyes go wide and I shoved him so he smacked square on his closed double doors.

"Fuck if I knew she was *your* mother!" I shoved him out of the way and tried to open the door but it seemed locked. I looked to Romeo and he stuck his tongue out at me, wiggling it in and out- showing the key in plain sight. I punched him in the chest and he put the key in his cheek, putting his arms against the doors behind me.

"You remember." He said simply and I stood there, wide eyed and silent. I didn't move, I didn't talk, and I didn't flinch. He took a step closer to kiss me on the lips but I moved my head to the side, clenching my jaw so it landed on my cheek.

"I need to go." He inched back a little bit and I faced him again, giving him a look of anger, but I didn't glare. I kept my jaw clenched and he clenched his as well, knowing what he did crossed my line. We stared at each other for a minute, the only sound I could hear was our breathing. He narrowed his eyes at me for a moment but then nodded, dropping his arms. He pulled a bobby pin out of the inside of his hair and shoved it in the lock, a click sounding from the door knob. I watched as he fumbled with it, his arm stretching across from me to do so. I looked back to him and he pulled a spitty key out of his mouth.

"It was a fake." He said and dropped it on the floor. I nodded and pulled the door open and took the same route down stairs. I heard the door shut and I descended the middle staircase. Meredith was frowning when I made it to the bottom.

"Sorry on behalf of my son, he can be rude and have no manners sometimes." *You bet.*

"Its okay, really, but we have to go. We have plans tonight." She nodded and I shook her hand, "The dinner was flawless and your house is amazing though. Thank You for inviting us." She nodded in response and I put on a light smile. She smiled as well and the other girls joined us in the living room.

"No problem, and call me if you still are interested. Monroe's never let a good adventure slip through their fingers just so easily." I nodded and pushed one of the flowers closer to my scalp so that it wouldn't fall out or go loose.

"Well, we will see the outcome." She smiled and led us to the door.

"Bye-bye, now." I said my goodbyes and made my way outside with the girls, as soon as the door shut the whispers between them started to erupt.

"What happened with Romeo?" Bambi asked quietly, I just shook my head slowly at her, watching my toes tap against the pavement as we made our way to the valet. The man stopped us with a hand in my face, and proceeded to interrupt us.

"Which one of you is Sarah Stewart?" Sarah raised her hand a little bit and he pointed to a car parked in the distance, she gasped and put a hand over her mouth.

"A young man is waiting for you in his car over there." Ivy smiled and nudged her to go but she stayed put.

"He has been starting to stalk me I think. I am afraid he gets violent with me sometimes and that is why I didn't want you to meet him. I have to go." I felt my hand enclose around her wrist and she snapped her head back.

"You can't just say something like that then leave. You're not going anywhere with him." She plastered a smile on her face, which seemed more frightening than happy looking. I felt fear for Sarah in a way a best friend only could. Raw emotion.

"Scarlett, let me go. I will talk to you later." She yanked her hand out of my grasp and I glanced back at the beat up black Cadillac. She trotted her way there and put on a believable smile for the boy as she opened up the door. It was dark outside so the only thing I could catch were the shine of his blue eyes reflecting off the porch lights. They narrowed at me and when I looked at Sarah one last time before she ducked into the car there were tears in her eyes. They puttered off and I felt my throat grow dry as the keys landed in Bambi's palm. I almost thought the chime of them echoed throughout the world. At least in my world they did.

# Chapter 33

The drive home felt solitary.

"She will be fine. She didn't tell us that he actually has abused her before." Bambi said softly from the side of me, driving. I chewed on my nails and watched out the window as raindrops streamed down, turning the lights outside into blurry circles of color.

"Still..." was all I could mutter. Ivy sighed in the back and I bit down on my skin. "What if he tries something?" I said, clenching my eyes shut trying not to think about it.

"She has a cell phone." Bambi said, clearing her throat and turning on the windshield wipers.

"Can we stop for a drink please? I need to go to the bathroom and a glass of water." Bambi nodded and pulled into a convenience store called *Pam's General Store*. She put some gas in her tank while I ran across the parking lot to get to the door. I grabbed a plastic cup and filled it with drinking fountain water, and then went to the ladies room and set the cup down on the sink. I picked a stall and went to the bathroom while someone else came into the bathroom. I saw through the crack of the door that it was someone tall and in a hood with layers on. They had something in their hand and they turned the faucet on, someone else came into the bathroom and picked a stall as well, throwing their jacket over the crack so I couldn't see what they were doing anymore.

The sink shut off and I pulled my dress down and my underwear up, quickly opening my stall door. It slammed against the wall and echoed through my ears as I was looking at an empty sink, unattended. I picked up my water and held it up to the light in case someone thought it would be funny to put pee or something in it. It seemed as crystal clear as when I first got it out of the fountain outside the bathroom. I shrugged, quickly washed my hands and grabbed my water, making my way out the car. They all sat inside waiting for me, the humming of the heat on I could hear all the way from the door. I sat inside and took a sip of my drink, a metallic aftertaste to it. Bambi handed me a pill that I recognized from the bottle she picked up at the hospital. "Take this." I nodded and set it at the back of my throat, the nasty taste of markers or something like that sticking to my tongue as I swallowed it down.

"Ugh." Bambi drove near the house and I sipped more and more of my drink, getting tired. Once we pulled in her driveway, they went inside and I asked for a couple minutes alone. I sat there in silence, my legs cold as hell. I drank the last of my water, crushed the cup and threw it aside in her car, telling myself I would pick it up later and apologize. I sighed then got out of the car, setting my foot out and standing up. I clicked my way up the walkway, but then something grabbed my from behind. I tried to scream out from the hand covering my mouth, but it was clamped hard on my mouth. I felt my muscles relax and my body slowly feel drowsy. I felt a pinch and my muffled out cries came silent and they kicked my legs to make me walk. My shins ached from the force of their boot and I fell asleep, someone dragging my feet against the road, watching the view of myself getting pulled slowly from Bambi's house was the last thing I ever saw before I blacked out.

The last thing I probably would ever see again.

# Chapter 34

"Scarlett!" I got slammed into from the side, and fell on the grass, leaves crumpling from under me. Heth was on top of me, stood up and grabbed my arm, pulling me up off the ground, frantic. "I have to show you something." I grumbled and followed him as he dragged me along, my feet barely touching the ground. His bare chest shown as he was just wearing some black sweat pants.

"Where are we going? And don't you ever wear a shirt?" He had a no-nonsense kind of attitude.

"Do you really want to put slits in every shirt I get? You can do that job. I have to show you something, come on!" I kept following him and stumbled from behind him, his arm still yanking me along. We stopped and I looked up. I looked at an all-too-familiar tombstone of an angel with wings rapping around himself. I read the name on it too, Heth Blakeley.

"Why are you showing me this?" I asked horrified, moving my hair over my shoulders so that he wouldn't look me strait in the face. The movement felt like a habit.

"This is the end. You see this?" He asked, his voice shaky- his hair falling into his eyes, his silver eyes filled with tears. He ran a hand over one of the wings on the grave. "This is the last life I have had before the one I have now. Except the one I have now, the body I inhabit...when I am there I don't really know I am me." He put a finger to his own chest.

"I don't really know that my spirit still roams..." He bit his lip, and then pursed his lips together and one tear fell. "I don't really know...that my spirit still follows *you*...and that I die every time because of *you*." I felt hot tears dripping from my face without even realizing it. I reached my hand out towards him and he took a step back.

"I-I don't understand, *je ne comprends vraiment pas.*" I put a hand over my mouth and shook my head. "I mean, 'I really do not understand'. Did I just speak French?" He took another step back, and shook his head.

"*You*," he pointed towards me and shook his head one more time, "Are the reason why I have experienced bereavement over and over and *over*." Another tear fell down his face, by the side of his nose. "Your reason why I am stuck in this afterlife." I shook my head in anguish, and all of a sudden everything slowed down. Heth Blakeley turned his back on me and started to run away from me, and I was too slow to catch him. I ran after him, never fast enough- he kept becoming smaller and smaller as he ran into the rising sun.

He became a speck and the brisk fall air became cold as my legs became more and more heavy, starting to push through snow which seemed to grow more and more feet from the leaf covered ground.

I could see my breath and my some of my hair fell off so that it was a couple inches shorter. It became chocolate brown and my lips became more soft and wet as I felt red lipstick on them. I stopped completely from all the elements holding me back when I saw a couple dots of red crimson blood on the snow in front of me. The snow went up to my mid thigh and I watched as two people in the distance stood, speaking. The boy with long brown hair had his arms in the air and I watched the morbid scene as blood dripped out of his chest a little more. He fell in the snow in slow motion and the other man dropped a bloody pocket knife to the ground and smiled down at his work.

"Thayer! Father, no! What have you done?" I heard myself scream, as I heard Thayer sink into the snow. The man who was my father didn't look at me. He just turned around slowly and watched a man, who I hadn't noticed before slowly clap for him. They both smiled in joy.

My legs didn't seem as heavy anymore, but the wind picked up, blowing snow all around, blurring the view of the three men in front of me, one dead. I pushed my way through towards them but the color of them started to fade away and I couldn't find the blood on the snow anymore.

The snow started to melt and the wind stopped as I ran as fast as I could forward, trying to catch something that I couldn't see. Everything became a little warmer and the sun shone high in the sky and the birds chirped. I ran slowly still, everything slowed down, and I saw a tree in front of my eyes.

I saw red apples all around the ground by the trunk and I watched in suffering as a man carried a sleeping man up a ladder and put the noose around his neck. I kept running towards them, not quick enough to stop him but watched as the man propped the red haired boy up in a sitting position on the ladder, climbed down then kicked the ladder out from underneath him. The boys eyes shot open and he struggled for a minute before finally exhaling his last breath. My long brown hair was suddenly curly and blond, my red lips turning into pale pink ones. I screamed in agony at the loss of the one I loved.

"Nolan! No, Father you killed him!" I sobbed quietly as the man who was supposed to be my father turned around to see a man nodding his head approvingly. I ran towards my father in an attempt to knock him over, hit him, kill him- anything, but the scene slowly started to change again. The people and the dead boy faded away and I kept running. I ran more and more and the flowers around me started to grow, the air grew more humid. I came to a barn where I ran inside the doors, and watched as a beautiful blond haired, grey eyed man, was beaten to death with a belt and a bat by my master, or as I put it- my father. He put his last lash on him before he went limp, bloody on the ground. My hair grew longer than ever, an onyx black shade over coming it.

"Heth! My love, no! You bastard, you murdered him!" I wailed, my knees growing painful and wobbly. I ran the other way, back out the doors, tears blurring my vision and I ran right into his tombstone again, the leaves under my feet trying to create some kind of wall or gate or barrier around the perimeter of the grave. Like it was trying so hard to protect the resting place of the reincarnated man I loved so much, but got killed every life he had.

114

He was so in love with me every chance he had, that he *died* for me every chance he had. I watched as the hard marble wings I wept on, became black and real. He stepped down from the tombstone and looked me hard in the eyes. "I was in love you. But you never gave me a chance to run away with you, Scarlett." I set my forehead on his chest, sobbing and wailing and crying hot tears. He stood there motionless, and I hit his chest lightly with my fist.

"I...am so-" I managed to get out but I was silenced by another sob ripping from my throat. "S-sorry! I am horrified! I got you killed, I should be killed!" I watched as my tears dripped down his chest. He stepped back from me.

"You will never die for me, I always die for you. That's just the way our lives are intertwined with each other." I fell to the ground and it started to rain, the cold water mixing with my salt water. He picked me up in his arms and kissed my lips lightly. "I am you guardian angel, even when I have fallen." I curled into his chest as water streamed from my hair and to the ground. I sobbed and sobbed as he carried me somewhere. "Its time that I don't die this time, I would like to stay with you for once in my life. I have to sacrifice someone else for you and I, and I am never that selfish so I guess that is my fault that I won't make the choice." I looked up at him.

"Then I will." He shook his head gravely and set me down at a tree, with a golden cup sitting in front of it. He grabbed the golden blade on a dark handled knife sitting in front of the cup and handed it to me. I cut my wrists and watched as the blood poured into the cup. Once it was half full, he put his thumbs to my cuts and closed his eyes, the wounds closing and healing all the way. I picked up the cup and handed it to him.

"Drink." He looked down at the cup and glanced at the blood pooling deep inside it. I watched him nervously as he set the cups edge to his lips, hesitated but then drank every last drop. After he drank it, I grabbed the cup out of his hands and threw it aside. I rapped my arms around his neck and kissed his bloodstained lips. I closed my eyes and a bright light exploded inside my head, and I could tell he was sharing the same feeling. My shoulders suddenly became sore and pain was shooting all through my body. His embrace was suddenly gone and everything was dark. I opened my eyes once again and found myself in reality. A whole different world than I was in.

I watched as Heth's spirit entered someone's body across the room, and they started to hack and cough. I suddenly knew why my shoulders were sore and my body was in pain.

My arms were above my head, my wrists were in chains that were cemented into the wall and my whole body was barely movable. I was in a dark room and there was a slight blue light coming from the bars about fifteen feet above my head. I saw that my dress was off, that I had a bra and underwear on but no shoes or anything else. My black hair was pooling over my front and I was shivering and my teeth were chattering. My eyes adjusted to the dark and I couldn't make out who was across the room from me, chained as well. I just saw that he was a man, as he had no shirt and just some fabric

115

covering his private parts. He was coughing and I heard a bang come from somewhere in the room. A lantern shone and a man came out of the dark holding it, setting it in the room, which I could only see his arm when he did. He finally stepped out of the shadows and the lantern light shone on who was sitting across from me. I felt my whole body go still as the two men revealed themselves.

Romeo was in chains on the other side of the room and most petrifying thing was who stepped out of the shadows.

Shane Kindle.

# Chapter 35

I couldn't have been more terrified in my whole entire life. I heard myself starting to whimper and desperately move as far away from Shane as possible. I scrambled back and Romeo, barely alive sit across from me, almost unconscious. He put his arms out as if he were introducing a show.

"My name is Vladimir Kindle, and welcome to my chambers." He chuckled darkly and I sat there, confused more than ever and more scared than I could have ever been. He took a step closer to me and smiled with bright white teeth.

"Y-your Shane." I stuttered, feeling the tears run down my face. I clenched my eyes shut.

"How about I give my new victims some background?" He laughed, clearly amused at our fear and agony. He leaned against the side of the wall in between the both of us and kept looking between me and Romeo as he spoke. "You see, I am *not* Shane Kindle." he almost spat in my face. "I am the unfortunate person who has gotten born with an identical twin brother. Shane, the stupid bastard, is that twin." He sneered and looked towards me. "If it weren't for the brotherly love I wouldn't have ever found you, now wouldn't I?" I felt myself suck in a breath, my hate for Shane sizzling down to nothing and my fear for myself and Romeo overpowering my emotion. "But don't worry I had more help with that, Sebastian!" My blank mind couldn't react fast enough, and as I heard that thump of the door being kicked open, I almost couldn't believe my eyes with what I saw.

"You called Vladimir?" He yelled before he opened the door and once he stepped through, Vladimir chortled.

"We have a royal guest for you." He said in a low tone and the man's face, when he saw who I was, was terror-stricken.

"S-sc..." was all he managed to get out, and I filled in the silence.

"Dad?" He put his hand to his mouth, seeing me with no clothes on and probably bruised.

"You did *not* touch my daughter!" He shouted at Vladimir and Vladimir's eyes grew wide and he pulled a gun out of his belt and pointed it at my dad's head.

"You *don't* raise your voice at me, Sebastian! You better think damn well of your actions before you end up dead." My dad nodded and I sat there in terror from the whole scene. He lowered the gun from his aim and put it back in his side pocket. Vladimir walked over to me and I screamed, scared out of my mind, not able to hold it back. He slapped me across the face and yelled at me. "*Shut the fuck up!*" I just kept sobbing silently as he messed with the shackles on my chains. "Stand!" I did as I was told and my arms screamed at me in protest. He pushed the chains up on a roller thing, and then locked it so that I would have to stand to keep myself up. He pulled out his gun and admired the shininess of the silver on it and I felt my whole body shake. He stepped back from me and leaned against the wall again. "So, Scarlett, what is it like to see your father after all this time?" He paused then smiled at me as if all of this was funny, "After that last time he molested you before he left you and Marion?" I kept my mouth shut. "Do you have anything to say to him?" He motioned for my dad to step closer to me so that we were a couple feet away from each other.

I coughed a little bit, gathered all my saliva and spat in his eye, all my phlegm and spit landing all over his face. "*That's* for my dead mother." He wiped his eye in surprise and shock and Vladimir laughed very hard.

"Shes testy, just like you, Sebastian!" He laughed some more and my dad wiped the rest of his face with his arm and stood there, silent.

I kicked him as hard as I could in the shins and he bent over in pain. "*Fuck you!*" I cringed as pain shot through my arms for tugging on them, and my legs for moving their muscled. Vladimir stepped in when he saw me getting violent and stroked my cheek with the back of his hand.

"Now, now, you have said all that is said. Or spat all that you have spat." He held back a laugh. "Bring in Sarah, would you? And tell her to bring the group." My dad tried his hardest not to limp his way out but he showed he was in pain. We all sat in silence, two of us in fear, as we waited. I thought about Sarah, wondering what he has done to her. I all of a sudden felt more afraid for her than me. My dad came in with others, but with a clump of Sarah's hair, dragging her in. He shoved her towards Vladimir and sat back in the shadows with the others, which of whom I couldn't see. She smiled, fake, and I glanced at her arms- the first thing I noticed, the first thing I feared.

Fingernail marks.

"Sarah, honey, look we have a guest." He pulled her into his arms and she put her head against his chest hesitantly, afraid. When she saw me her eyes grew wide and her dark irises highlighted the dry mascara trails running down her face, just like in my dream too, the only difference was that she was still a young girl, and hasn't aged or smoked. That was what I was aware of at the least.

"That's great darling." she said, her face screwed up in pain as I noticed his fingers digging into her arm as he embraced her. His nails were long and sharp and she had tears in her eyes as he caused her more and more pain. I didn't notice the marks before, she probably covered them up with makeup. He giggled in joy, purely excited.

"We have too many guests though, meaning we have to get rid of some. Boo!" He frowned and faked his sadness, grabbing his gun out of his pocket and motioning for the line to form. Random people stepped up, their heads held high so that they died with dignity. The last one that lined up saw me then he became alarmed more than everything. Hidalgo's lip trembled as he saw me and I started to sob quietly, knowing I was about to witness these people's deaths, especially the boy who I was about to start a relationship with.

I had my head hung low in grief for them, and jumped when the first gunshot went off. Everyone broke then and started to cry as one by one, he shot each of them in the

118

head. I counted off fourteen gunshots and then raised my head when he didn't shoot another time. I saw Hidalgo, the last one standing, horrified, looking away from the dead citizens that lay on the ground beside his feet. The blood seeping through his shoes, before running down the drain.

"Hidalgo, come here." He walked toward him and Vladimir shoved Sarah aside so that he grabbed him by his hair. I watched, screaming at the top of my lungs as he took a butcher knife out from his belt and held it up to his neck.

"No! Stop, please!" I screamed and pleaded but he didn't budge. Sarah turned her face into the blue brick wall and looked away as she knew what was about to happen.

"Scarlett- looks at me!" He laughed and yelled from the top of his lungs, adrenaline pumping from all the things he just did. "I made a phrase, just for you, just so you can remember the words as I *kill* this man!" He laughed one more time and I heard Hidalgo whisper to me before Vladimir continued.

"I love you, Scarlett." Hidalgo said almost silently and I cried even more and tried to free my wrists from the chains, to no avail.

"Why don't we just nip this in the-" Vladimir started, then I watched as he dug the knife in Hidalgo's throat, and I heard the loudest scream ever come from my throat as I heard the gurgling sound come from his mouth, "*Blood!*" He let go of his hair and let Hidalgo fall to the ground dead, right in front of my eyes. He grabbed Sarah and shoved my dad out the door, leaving me standing there wailing and crying for the boy that lay dead in front of my feet.

I was going to die, everyone is going to die.

I couldn't take the pressure of reality, and just then I felt myself go weak in the knees as I fell to my fate.

The fate of my soon-to-be death.

# Epilogue

*"Investigation and Search for Two Women, One Man Gone Missing"*

On Tuesday, March 23rd, two women and one man, all age 22, Scarlett Tod, Sarah Stewart and Romeo Monroe, went missing at about 10:30 PM when visiting for dinner at Meredith Monroe, mother of Romeo Monroe's house. Meredith has recently been put on trial as well as Bambi Edwards and Ivy Stables for the case of the missing adults, and all three have been questioned. When we attempted to interview Ms. Edwards and Ms. Stables they responded with no comment. Ms. Monroe however wanted to state her placing in the whole case. Meredith responded when we asked if she was responsible for the missing existence of her son she stated, "I would never lay a hand on my son, just because we don't spend a lot of time together do to my work does not mean that I would hurt him. As it goes for the other two girls, I said my goodbyes once they left the door of my house and that was the last I ever saw of them. I have nothing to do with their missing trials." It is said that she has gotten an attorney to speak on her behalf and that she has paid thousands of dollars for detectives for her son. But when it comes to Sarah Stewart and Scarlett Tod, she has no place in helping their investigation. The search is still going and we will be posting weekly about this case.

MIX
Papier | Fördert
gute Waldnutzung
FSC® C083411

Zeitfracht Medien GmbH
Ferdinand-Jühlke-Straße 7
99095 Erfurt, Deutschland
produktsicherheit@kolibri360.de

Druck:
CPI Druckdienstleistungen GmbH
im Auftrag der
Zeitfracht Medien GmbH
Ein Unternehmen der Zeitfracht - Gruppe
Ferdinand-Jühlke-Str. 7
99095 Erfurt